# The Library of Wonder

By Lizy J Campbell

To everyone who believes in the magic of libraries and their importance to stay within our communities.

-L. J Campbell

# Prologue

The library door behind her creaks, then slowly, as if moved by an invisible hand, it shuts closed with a heavy thud.

The flickering light of her old pocket flashlight bobbed along as she walked, the silence of the abandoned building amplifying every little noise.

She roams from aisle to aisle, her eyes wide as she scans the titles of ancient tomes, wondering if any of them had magic hidden inside. And that's when she saw *the* book. It didn't glow or hum, but it had this strange, magnetic pull, nestled all alone on a crooked shelf.

Emma reaches for it without hesitation.

As soon as her fingers wrap around the spine, a loud crack echoes through the library. The entire shelf rattles violently, and the floor beneath her feet shifts.

"What the.." Emma begins, but before she can finish, the whole shelf *lurches* forward. Books tumble down like an avalanche of paper and ink, and Emma did what anyone in her position would do: she shrieked.

But that wasn't the worst part.

No, the worst part was when one of the books flung open midair and sucked her into it like a vacuum cleaner gone mad.

One moment, Emma was standing in the library, and the next...*whoosh!* She is tumbling through the air, falling through what looks like a swirling tornado of flying letters and commas, punctuation marks zipping past her head.

"This can't be real!" Emma shouts, flailing her arms as she spins like a ragdoll. "I was just.. *AHHHHHHHH!*"

With a loud *thud*, she landed face-first on a hard, cobblestone street. The ground wobbled beneath her as if the entire world was made of jelly.

Dazed, Emma slowly sat up, blinking rapidly at her surroundings.

"Am I... in a *book*?" she asks aloud, staring at the strange town.

# Chapter 1: The Great Jellybean Chase

The library was ancient, its stone walls gray and crumbling from age. It stood at the edge of town, quiet and unassuming, like a forgotten secret. It had been closed for years. Emma had passed it every day, never imagining that it would become the most important place in her life; or the most dangerous.

The moon hung low in the sky, casting long shadows across the wet cobblestone streets of downtown Guildford, England.

It was November 14th, the fallen leaves were blowing in the wind, sending a chill right down to her bones. Emma had no real home to return to, and no family to miss her. She wandered the streets aimlessly, her hands tucked deep in the pockets of her thin worn-out frayed coat, her failed attempt at trying to keep her frail hands warm.

*That's when she saw it.*

The blue peeled painted door to the library was slightly ajar, a soft golden light spilled out into the night. The warmth from within she could feel it, like it was inviting her in from the cold. Emma had always loved books, each one a world that offered an escape, even if it was just for a little while. Emma poked her head inside.

The air was thick with the scent of old paper and dust, but there was something else, something strange. The shelves were humming softly, as if alive, and the books were pulsing with life, mimicking her heartbeat. The only sound was the distant ticking of a clock bell, chiming.

*Midnight.*

Sneaking into the abandoned library at night was *definitely* not one of Emma's brightest ideas. But then again, Emma didn't always think things through.

The orphanage had its rules, very strict, boring rules. And one of the most important ones was: *"No running away or wandering the town."* But how could Emma resist the old library, after overhearing rumors about the strange place. The door left just *slightly* ajar.

"It's not breaking in if the door is already open, right," Emma whispers to herself, as if that made it any less sneaky or wrong.

Emma grins. "I am home," she mutters.

---

One minute Emma was standing in the library looking around, and then she touched one of the glowing books. *Poof!*

She was no longer in the old musty library.

Instead, she was in the middle of a strange town square. Shops with crooked signs are leaned haphazardly on either side of her, and the sky overhead was a swirling mix of purple and orange, like someone had painted it with leftover watercolors.

"Great. I didn't just fall into a book," Emma groans, rubbing her head. "I fell into the *weirdest* book ever."

As if on cue, a large purple duck wearing a tiny top hat, waddles past her. The duck tipped its hat and quacks, "Good evening, young miss."

Emma stares at the duck in disbelief; her mouth open. "Of course. Talking animals."

Before she could even begin to process the situation, a group of juggling teen squirrels wearing tutus run by, followed by an orange rabbit on roller skates shouting, "Make way! Make way!"

"This... is officially... the strangest thing I have ever seen. Great I have completely lost my mind," Emma mumbles to herself, standing up and brushing the dirt from her tattered clothes.

Suddenly, a voice behind her pipes up. "You there! You're new, aren't you?"

Emma turns around to find an impatient-looking owl dressed in business attire, perched on a lamppost, peering down at her over the rim of a pair of tiny spectacles. The owl sighs dramatically. "Another one, I see. Well, don't just stand there, you'll miss the story! Hurry, before it starts without you."

Emma blinks. "Excuse me?"

The owl flutters its wings in exasperation. "Oh dear, one of *those* types. Look, you fell into a book as it happens. Now, if you don't want to be stuck here forever, you'd better follow the plot."

Emma's heart skips a beat. "Stuck? Forever, um.. what plot?"

The owl nods gravely. "Forever. Unless you find the enchanted bookmark to take you back. Now, follow along, there's no time to waste! The story waits for no one."

Emma's mind races. "Enchanted book-mark? Are you kidding me? This is a nightmare!"

The owl shrugs. "I don't write the rules, I just squawk them."

Before Emma could argue further, the owl takes off into the sky, leaving her standing in the middle of this ridiculous town square. "Well, this is just perfect," she mutters to herself. "How on earth am I going to explain this one?" Emma's mind whirling.

A whisper in the wind sends a chill down her spine.

*'Return before dawn,'* it says, *'or be lost forever.'*

Emma still couldn't believe it. She was actually inside a book. Not just *reading* a book, oh no, that would be too simple. She was *living* it. And from what the impatient owl had told her, if she didn't play along, she'd be stuck here. *Forever.*

"Of all the books to fall into," she muttered, kicking a pink pebble down the cobblestone street. "Why couldn't it have been a book about superheroes or dragons? But no, I'm in a town where the ducks wear hats and talk!"

As if to remind her, the same duck from earlier waddled past her again, tipping its hat with a polite "Quack quack, madam." Emma groaned.

She didn't know where she was supposed to go or what she was supposed to do. The town around her looked like something out of a children's story gone completely bonkers. There were animals talking, juggling squirrels, and for some reason, a candy store in every corner. The air even smelled faintly of sugar and peppermint.

A sign caught her eye: *Jolly Joe's Jellybean Emporium.*

"Well, if I'm stuck in a weird candy town, I might as well get some snacks," Emma said, shrugging as she pushed open the door. Her belly grumbled in agreement. A bell jingled overhead as she walked in.

Inside, the shelves were filled with jars of colorful jellybeans, stacked from floor to ceiling.

Behind the counter stood a very round man with a long black handlebar mustache and a yellow chef's hat, who looked absolutely delighted to see her.

"Ah, welcome to the finest jellybean shop in all of Sugartown!" he boomed. "What's your pleasure? Pineapple? Popcorn? Pickle-flavored?"

Emma raised an eyebrow. "Pickle?"

The man winked. "For the daring, of course! Now, what'll it be?"

Before Emma could respond, a tiny, giggling creature darted past her legs, swiping a handful of jellybeans from one of the jars. The creature looked like a miniature green rabbit, except its ears were too long, and it wore red striped socks.

"Hey!" Emma called after it. "That thing just stole your jellybeans!"

The shopkeeper waved it off with a chuckle. "Oh, that's just a Jellybean Jumper. Mischievous little fellow. But harmless. Well... mostly harmless."

"Mostly?" Emma repeated.

The Jellybean Jumper zipped around the room, scattering jellybeans everywhere, laughing like a maniac. Emma ducked as a handful of jellybeans flew past her head. "What happens if it's not harmless?"

The shopkeeper shrugged. "They've been known to cause a bit of chaos from time to time. But nothing to worry about! Although..." He leaned in closer, his voice dropping to a whisper. "Legend has it that if you can catch a Jellybean Jumper, it will lead you to something special."

Emma raised an eyebrow. "Something special? Like what?"

The shopkeeper's eyes twinkled. "Oh, you know, the usual... enchanted bookmarks, magical keys, portals to other worlds. That sort of thing."

Emma's heart skipped a beat. "Did you say *enchanted bookmark*?"

He nodded. "But you'll have to catch the little rascal first."

Emma turned just in time to see the Jellybean Jumper zip out the door, leaving a trail of jellybeans behind. She didn't even hesitate. If this creature could lead her to the enchanted bookmark, she had no choice but to chase it.

With a burst of speed, Emma sprinted out of the shop and down the street, dodging other townsfolk and hopping over the occasional candy wrapper.

"Come back here!" she shouted, her arms flailing above her head as she tried to keep up with the Jumper. It zigzagged through the crowd, bouncing off walls spinning around lampposts, and dropping jelly beans everywhere! Every time Emma got close, it darted away, giggling like a sugar-crazed wacko.

It led her through a park, around a fountain shaped like a giant lollipop, and then, finally, into an alley that seemed quieter than the rest of the town. The Jumper stopped, perched on top of a large jellybean-shaped rock, staring at her with its beady orange little eyes.

Emma, panting and completely out of breath, bent over and glared at it. "Okay... you win... you're fast... but now... what?"

The Jumper tilted its head, then, with surprising calmness, held out a tiny paw. Dangling from its fingers was a shimmering silver bookmark, glowing faintly with golden threads woven into its surface.

Emma's eyes widened. "Is that...?"

The Jumper nodded, still grinning.

Carefully, Emma reached out and took the bookmark. The moment her fingers touched it, the bookmark sparkled brightly, and a wave of warmth washed over her. She could feel its magic humming in her hand, like it was alive.

"Thank you," she whispered, but the Jellybean Jumper had already bounced off, disappearing into the shadows with a final giggle.

Emma looked down at the enchanted bookmark, realizing what this meant. She had found it, the key to getting out of this ridiculous story and back to the library.

She could feel the pull of the bookmark, urging her to read the next book.

Taking a deep breath, Emma tucked the bookmark into her pocket and stood up.

"Well," she said to herself, glancing back at the strange town one last time. "I guess it's time to turn the page as they say."

And with that oddly enough, the world around her swirled into light once again, as she was whisked away back to the library.

---

# Chapter 2: The Library That Shouldn't Be

The orphanage was never truly home. It was a place where days bled into nights, where faces came and went, and the only constant was the knowledge that no one was coming to save you. Emma had spent twelve years of her life waiting for something to change, for someone, anyone to claim her, but no one ever did.

Emma wandered deeper into the library, her fingers grazing the spines of the books as she passed. Titles jumped out at her: *Tales of the Forgotten*, *The Lost Kingdom of Amaranth*, *Echoes of the Past*. Each one seemed to pulse with a quiet individual energy, like they were alive somehow, waiting to be discovered.

A light flickered in the far corner of the room and drew Emma's attention. She moved closer, and realized it was coming from a single book on a pedestal, its cover glowing faintly in the darkness. Unlike the other books, this one looked new, untouched by time. The leather was smooth, its edges sharp, and engraved in gold on the cover were words in a language Emma couldn't read.

Her hand hovered above it, a sense of wonder and fear swirling inside her. She didn't know why, but something about this book felt important.

Before she could stop herself, Emma reached out and touched the cover.

The world around her shifted once more.

The floor vanished from beneath her feet, and she was falling—falling into darkness, into nothingness. Emma tried to scream, but no sound came out of her mouth. The air was thick, pressing in on her from all sides, suffocating her. Just as panic had begun to set in, a burst of light exploded in front of her, and suddenly, she was no longer in the library.

She was standing in the middle of a dense forest.

Tall trees with silver bark stretched up toward the sky, their leaves shimmering like tiny stars. The air was cool and crisp, filled with the sound of rustling leaves and distant birdsong. Emma spun around, her heart pounding in her chest. This wasn't possible. One minute she had been in the library, and now...

*This all has to be a dream*, she thought. *It has to be.*

But everything felt too real. The soft earth beneath her feet, the cool breeze on her face. She reached out and touched the nearest tree, half expecting her hand to pass through it, but the bark was solid, and rough against her skin.

*This was real too.*

Emma's mind raced, trying to make sense of it all. Where was *here*? Her thoughts were interrupted by a low growl from behind her. She froze in terror. Slowly, she turned around.

A creature stood at the edge of the trees, its eyes glowing red in the shadows. It was like nothing Emma had ever seen before; part wolf, part shadow, its body shifting and twisting as if it were made of smoke. The growl deepened, and the creature took a step toward her.

Fear surged through Emma, her heart hammering in her chest. She backed away, but the creature followed, its eyes locked on her with deadly intent. She needed to run, to get away, but her feet felt rooted to the ground, as if the forest itself was holding her in place.

*Move,* she told herself. *Move!*

With a burst of adrenaline, Emma turned and bolted into the trees, her legs pumping as fast as they could carry her. The creature let out a piercing howl, and she could hear it crashing through the underbrush behind her. She didn't dare look back. Branches whipped at her face, tearing at her clothes, but she didn't slow down. She couldn't.

Her lungs burned, and her legs ached, but still, she ran. The forest seemed to stretch on forever, an endless maze of silver trees and shadows. Panic clawed at her mind. There was no way out. She was going to die here, in this strange, impossible place.

Suddenly, the ground beneath her gave way, and Emma tumbled down a steep embankment, her body rolling and crashing through the underbrush. She hit the bottom with a hard thud, the wind knocked out of her. Dazed and breathless, she lay there for a moment, staring up at the sky.

The creature's growls echoed from above, but they didn't follow. It stayed at the top of the embankment, pacing back and forth, its red eyes glowing in the darkness. Emma's heart raced as she watched it, her body trembling with fear. Why wasn't it coming after her?

She didn't have time to wonder. The ground beneath her began to tremble, and the air filled with a strange humming sound. Emma scrambled to her feet, her eyes darting around in panic.

A large stone structure stood in the clearing ahead, half-buried in the earth. It looked like an old, crumbling doorway, covered in vines and moss. But there was something about it that felt... familiar. As if she had seen it before, in a dream or an old, buried memory.

The humming grew louder, and the doorway began to glow with a soft, golden light. Emma's breath caught in her throat. This was it. This was her way out, hopefully, even out of the library.

Without hesitation, she ran toward the doorway, her feet pounding against the earth. The creature let out a furious snarl from behind her, but it was too late. Emma reached the doorway and threw herself through it just as the world around her exploded in a blinding flash of light.

Everything was white.

Then, slowly,  when the light began to fade, Emma found herself back in the library. She was lying on the cold and cracked old stone floor, her body aching from the fall. The golden light that emanated from the book had disappeared, leaving the room in nothing but dark shadows.

She lay there for a long moment, her mind reeling and contemplating everything that had just happened. Her hand brushed against something cold and smooth, and she looked down.

The book was still there, its cover now dull and lifeless and aged like the library itself. She stared at it, and something inside her shifted. This wasn't just a dream. This was real. The library had shown her something important.

Slowly, Emma got to her feet, her legs shaking and cold. She glanced around the library, half-expecting the creature from the forest to appear before her, but everything was eerily quiet. The shelves still loomed above her, dark and ominous.

With one last glance at the now-quiet book, Emma put the book back on the shelf, turned and walked deeper into the library.

# Chapter 3: Whispers in the Dark

The further Emma ventured into the library, the golden glow was replaced by a dim, flickering light that barely illuminated the path ahead.

The air had grown colder, and Emma hugged her arms to her chest, her breath coming in uneven gasps. The vast, towering shelves felt like walls were closing in on her.

The memory of the forest, the creature, and the strange doorway lingered in her mind, refusing to fade. But her body ached from the fall, and the dirt still clung to her clothes, proof that whatever had happened, it wasn't just her imagination.

The silence in the library was oppressive. Even her footsteps seemed muffled, absorbed by the heavy, watchful air. Emma stopped for a moment, listening. There was no sounding ticking of clocks, no creak of old wood, not even the faint rustle of pages. It was as if the entire building was holding its breath, waiting.

And then she heard it. A whisper, faint and distant, like a voice carried off in the wind.

*"Return... before dawn..."*

Emma's heart leapt into her throat. She spun around, searching for the source of the voice, but the library remained still, unchanged. The whisper had been so soft, so fleeting, that for a moment, she thought she had imagined it. But the words lingered in her mind, cold and insistent.

*"Return... before dawn..."*

A heavy knot of anxiety twisted in her stomach. The library wasn't just some strange, magical place where stories came to life. It had ruled that Emma was just beginning to understand. And one of those rules, the most important, was that she couldn't stay here forever. She had to leave. But how? And what would happen if she didn't?

Emma took a deep breath, her fingers trembling slightly as she ran them along the spines of the books on the nearest shelf. Each one was old and weathered, its title barely visible under layers of dust. She pulled the book free and opened it, but the pages were blank—every single one of them. Her heart sank. She tried another book, then another, but each was the same. Blank. Empty.

The pull she had felt moments ago began to twist into something darker, something more ominous. This library wasn't just a place to read stories; it was a puzzle, a riddle she had to solve. And if she didn't, if she couldn't find the way out before dawn...

*Return before dawn*, the whisper had said.

Emma's mind raced. Dawn wasn't far away. How long had she been here? There were no clocks, no windows, no way to measure time. But she could feel the weight of it pressing down on her, slipping away with every second she wasted.

"I need to find a way out," she whispered to herself, her voice shaking. "There *has* to be a way out."

As she moved further into the library, the shelves grew narrower, the books older and more worn. The smell of musty paper grew stronger, and the light seemed to dim even more, until she could barely see the floor beneath her feet. But still, she pressed on, driven by the need to understand what was happening, to find the answers hidden in the pages around her.

She came to a sudden stop when she reached a large, circular clearing in the center of the library. In the middle of the clearing was a pedestal, much like the one she had seen before, but this one was different. Instead of a single book, there were three.

Each one was glowing faintly, their covers marked with strange symbols that Emma didn't recognize. She approached cautiously, her heart pounding in her chest. There was something about these books that felt important. It was as if the library was guiding her to them, offering her a clue, a way forward.

But which one should she choose?

The whisper echoed in her mind again, louder this time.

*"Return... before dawn..."*

Emma glanced around, her eyes scanning the shadows for any sign of movement, but the library remained eerily still. Her fingers hovered over the first book, a thick, leather-bound tome with a symbol that looked like an hourglass etched into the cover. Time. Could this book hold the answers to how much time she had left? To how she could escape before dawn?

Her hand moved to the second book, smaller and worn, with a symbol that resembled a key. A key to unlock something, the door that had trapped her here? Something even deeper, something hidden within the library itself.

The third book was different from the others. It was thin, almost fragile, and its cover was marked with a single eye. Emma felt a shiver run down her spine as she looked at it. The eye watched her, its gaze piercing and knowing. This book felt dangerous, like it held secrets that should never be uncovered.

Emma hesitated, her mind swirling with uncertainty. Time was running out. She could feel it slipping away, like sand through her fingers. She had to make a choice. But which book would lead her to the truth? Which one would help her escape?

*Trust your instincts*, a voice whispered in her mind—her own voice, this time.

Emma's hand hovered over the second book, the one with the key. Something about it felt right. It wasn't the largest or the most imposing of the three, but there was a quiet power in it, a sense that it held the answers she needed. With a deep breath, she reached out and picked it up.

As soon as her fingers touched the cover, the library shifted again. The air grew heavier, and the floor beneath her feet seemed to ripple like water. Emma stumbled back, clutching the book to her chest, as the shadows around her deepened. For a moment, she thought she had made the wrong choice, that the library was punishing her.

But then, the pedestal began to sink into the floor, disappearing into the ground with a soft rumble. The shelves around her seemed to bend and warp, their edges blurring as if the library itself was changing, rearranging. And then, just as suddenly as it had started, everything went still.

Emma stood in the center of the clearing, her heart racing, the book still clutched tightly in her hands. The library was quiet again, but the silence felt different now. It wasn't the heavy, watchful silence from before. This was an expectant silence, as if the library was waiting for her to take the next step.

Emma opened the book.

The pages were filled with strange symbols and ruins, none of which she could read. Her heart sank. Was this just another dead end? Another trick? She flipped through the pages, her fingers trembling with frustration. And then she saw it.

A single line of text, written in a language she could understand:

*"The door to the past is unlocked by the key to memory."*

Emma stared at the words, her mind racing. The door to the past? What did that mean? And what was the key to her memory? She thought back to the strange doorway in the forest, the one she had stumbled through to escape the creature.

Could that have been the door to the past? Or was it something else, something deeper within the library itself?

The pull in her chest grew stronger, more insistent. The library wanted her to understand, to figure out the puzzle.

*"Return... before dawn..."*

The whisper was louder now, echoing through the library, filling the air with a sense of urgency. Emma's heart raced. She needed to find the way out. She needed to understand the puzzle before it was too late.

Suddenly, a soft light flickered to life at the far end of the clearing, drawing Emma's attention. It was a doorway, just like the one in the forest, but this one was different. It was glowing with a soft, golden light, and the air around it seemed to hum with energy.

Emma's breath caught in her throat. This was it. This was the door she needed to go through. The door to the past.

But even as she took a step toward it, a cold voice whispered in her ear:

*"Not yet..."*

Emma froze, her heart pounding in her chest. The voice wasn't the same as the whisper from before. This one was darker, colder, filled with malice. She glanced around, her eyes searching the shadows for the source of the voice, but there was nothing there. Just darkness.

*"Not yet..."* the voice repeated, closer this time, as if it were right behind her.

Emma spun around, her pulse racing. Her eyes darted around the library, but everything was still. Too still. She backed away, her fingers tightening around the book. She had to leave. She had to get out before it was too late.

But the pull was stronger than ever now, pulling her toward the glowing doorway. She couldn't resist it. She had to go through. She had to find the answers.

With a deep breath, Emma stepped toward the door, her heart pounding in her chest. She reached out, her fingers brushing against the glowing surface.

And then the world exploded in light.

For a moment, Emma was blind, her body weight

less as she was pulled through the doorway. The air around her shimmered and rippled, and she could feel the library shifting again, the walls and shelves bending and warping as the world changed.

And then, just as suddenly, she was standing in a new place.

The air was thick with the scent of saltwater and smoke. The ground beneath her feet was rough and uneven, like cobblestones worn smoothly by years of use. Emma blinked, her eyes adjusting to the dim light, and realized she was standing in the middle of an old, crumbling courtyard. The sky above her was dark, filled with swirling clouds of ash and smoke, and in the distance, she could hear the faint crash of waves against rocks.

This was no ordinary place. It felt old, ancient, like a forgotten piece of the past.

And then she saw a figure, standing at the far end of the courtyard, shrouded in shadow.

"Emma..." the figure whispered; its voice barely audible above the wind.

Emma's heart raced. How did it know her name? Who—no, *what*—was it?

She took a cautious step forward, the book still clutched in her hands, as the figure began to move toward her. The pull in her chest grew stronger, almost painful now, as if the library itself was urging her toward the figure, urging her to understand.

But there was something else, something darker. The cold, whispering voice from before echoed in her mind, a warning she didn't fully understand.

"Not yet..."

Emma stopped, her breath catching in her throat. She didn't know what to do. The figure was getting closer, its movements slow and deliberate, as if it had all the time in the world.

But she didn't.

The words from the book echoed in her mind: *The door to the past is unlocked by the key to memory.*

Was this the past? Was this the key?

Emma's heart pounded in her chest as the figure came closer, its face still hidden in shadow. She had to make a choice, stay, and face whatever was coming or turn and run.

The pull in her chest told her to stay.

But the cold voice whispered: *"Not yet..."*

# Chapter 4: Shadows of the Past

Emma stands frozen, her breath shallow and rapid, fingers trembling around the edges of the worn book she clutches to her chest. The figure in the distance moves toward her, and with every step, the strange pull in her chest intensifies. She wants to run, everything in her screams to help her feet stay rooted in place. Something, or someone, is holding her here. The library isn't done with her yet.

Her clothes, tattered and frayed from years of neglect, hang loose around her thin frame. The oversized coat she wears, its pockets filled with tiny trinkets she's collected over the years, is more a comfort than a shield against the cold. Her shoes are falling apart, one of them held together by a strip of torn fabric she found behind the orphanage weeks ago. Strands of dirty blonde hair fall into her eyes as she glances nervously at the approaching figure.

For a moment, Emma feels small, and insignificant. But then she remembers something about herself, something buried beneath the layers of dirt and exhaustion. She's always been a fighter. Maybe not with fists or words, but in her heart. She's resilient, stubborn in ways that no one ever really understood at the orphanage. She's the girl who, despite having nothing, always manages to hold on to hope. Even now, in this strange, terrifying place, she refuses to let fear swallow her whole.

She wipes her hand on her stained thin coat, trying to stop it from shaking, and steps forward.

"I'm not afraid," she whispers, trying to convince herself as much as anything. But the figure keeps moving, its face hidden by shadow, its form just a silhouette against the unnatural sky. She can't make out any details, and that makes her stomach twist with dread. But still, something inside her urges her forward.

Emma's eyes flicker down to the book in her hands. The cover is cool to the touch, the key symbol etched into it faintly glowing now. She knows this book holds answers, but she's not sure she wants to know what those answers are. Still, she flips it open again, her fingers moving quickly over the strange symbols and runes.

*The key to memory.* She rolls the phrase over in her mind, trying to make sense of it. Is it literal? Does she need to remember something? Or is there an actual key hidden in one of the library's forgotten corners, waiting for her to find it?

The figure is closer now, no more than a few yards away, its movement deliberate but slow, like it has all the time in the world. Emma's breathing quickens, and she forces herself to focus on the book again, flipping through the pages faster now, searching for anything else that might make sense. Blank pages fill her vision, over and over, until suddenly, her fingers catch onto a page that feels different.

The texture is smoother, newer. She stops, staring down at a page that wasn't there before. This one isn't blank. It's filled with intricate drawings; tiny, delicate sketches of doors. Hundreds of them. Some look grand and imposing, others small and almost hidden in their frames. But each one is unique, and Emma's heart skips a beat as she looks at them. One door, near the bottom corner of the page, looks exactly like the door she saw in the forest, the one she stumbled through to escape the creature.

Her fingers trace the outline of the door in the sketch, and as she does, the image seems to ripple, the paper beneath her hand softening, shifting. Before her eyes, the door begins to glow faintly, the lines becoming clearer, sharper, until the entire page pulses with light. Emma gasps, stepping back, the book still in her hands. It's as if the book is alive, responding to her touch, revealing itself only when it's ready.

The figure has stopped now, just a few feet away, standing at the edge of the clearing. Emma feels its eyes on her, though she can't see its face. The air between them is thick with tension, and she knows, deep down, that this figure is part of the puzzle, part of the library's twisted game.

She straightens her back, determination flickering in her chest. If the library wants her to play, she'll play. But she'll do it on her terms.

"What do you want?" she calls out, her voice echoing strangely in the quiet space. Her hands grip the book tighter as she steps toward the figure, refusing to let fear hold her back.

For a long moment, there's no response. The figure stands there, silent, and unmoving, its shadow stretching across the ground like a dark stain. And then, slowly, it raises its head.

The shadows peel away, revealing a face Emma recognizes.

It's her own.

Emma stumbles back, her breath catching in her throat. She's staring at herself, but it's not right. This version of her looks older, more worn down. There are deep lines etched into her face, her eyes hollow and dark, her clothes even more ragged and torn than Emma's own. The older Emma's mouth twists into a faint, sad smile, and when she speaks, her voice is soft, almost fragile.

"You can't leave," the older Emma says, her voice barely above a whisper. "Not yet."

Emma shakes her head, trying to process what she's seeing. This can't be real. It has to be some kind of illusion, a trick. But the older Emma steps closer, and the sadness in her eyes is all too real.

"You're not ready," the older Emma continues. "The library won't let you go until you understand."

"Understand what?" Emma's voice cracks. "What does the library want from me?"

The older Emma doesn't answer right away. Instead, she reaches out, her hand hovering just above the glowing book in Emma's hands. For a moment, the two of them stand there, connected by the faint glow of the book, their reflections of each other blurring in the dim light. And then, slowly, the older Emma speaks again.

"The library is a place of stories," she says quietly. "But not just any stories. It holds the past, the future... everything. But it also holds secrets:

secrets about who you are, about who you've been, and who you're supposed to become."

Emma feels a cold knot form in her stomach. She doesn't want to hear this. She doesn't want to believe it. But the pull in her chest grows stronger, more insistent, and she knows the older Emma is right. There's something here, something buried deep within the library, and she won't be able to leave until she finds it.

"But I don't even know what I'm looking for," Emma says, her voice small and lost. "How am I supposed to solve this if I don't even know what the puzzle is?"

The older Emma's eyes soften, and for the first time, she looks vulnerable; like she understands exactly how lost and scared Emma feels.

"You'll know," the older Emma whispers. "When the time comes, you'll know."

Before Emma can ask anything else, the older version of her fades away, dissolving into the shadows as if she was never really there. The clearing is empty again, the silence heavier than ever.

Emma stands there for a long time, the book still glowing faintly in her hands. Her mind races with questions, her chest tight with fear and confusion. She can't leave. Not until she understands.

But what does that even mean? What is the library hiding from her?

She flips through the book again, her eyes scanning the drawings of doors, the strange symbols that fill the pages. There's something she's supposed to remember, something she's forgotten. And the library won't let her go until she finds it.

But where does she even start?

Emma's hands shake as she closes the book and shoves it into the deep pocket of her coat. She needs to keep moving. She needs to figure this out. There's no time to waste. Dawn is coming, and if she doesn't find a way out before then...

She pushes the thought away and starts walking again, her steps quick and determined. The shelves stretch endlessly around her, the walls of books towering above her like the bars of a cage. But she refuses to let the fear control her. She's going to solve this. She's going to get out.

As she walks, her mind drifts to the past, the life she had before the library before the orphanage. She was so young when her parents died, too young to remember much. But there's one memory that stands out, a memory she's held on to all these years, like a tiny flame in the darkness.

She remembers her mother's voice, soft and warm, telling her stories before bed. Stories about magic and adventure, about faraway lands, and brave heroes. Emma would listen with wide eyes, her heart soaring with excitement and wonder. Those stories were her escape, her way of believing that there was something more out there, something beyond the walls of the orphanage.

But there was one story her mother told her more than any other. It was a story about a girl who could travel between worlds, who could step onto the pages of any book and become part of the story. Emma had always loved that story, but now, standing here in the library, she realizes that it wasn't just a story. It was a warning. A clue.

Her mother knew about the library.

Emma stops dead on tracks, her breath catching in her throat. Would it be possible? Could her mother have known about this place? The idea sends a jolt of electricity through her. Her mother's story wasn't just a bedtime tale, it was a piece of the puzzle. But why didn't she tell Emma the truth? Did she know Emma would end up here?

*"The key to memory,"* Emma whispers to herself, her fingers gripping the edges of her coat pocket where the book now rests. Her past, her mother's stories, are connected to this library. The

answers she's been searching for are tied to the very thing she's been running from her whole life: her own history.

Her heart races as she moves forward again, her eyes scanning the endless rows of books, searching for something that might lead her closer to the truth. The shelves seem to go on forever, the towering walls of books stretching into the shadows. But now she feels a strange certainty. The library wants her to find something, to unlock a piece of herself she's kept buried.

As she walks, her thoughts drift back to her childhood. She was only five when her parents died, and the details of that day are hazy at best. She remembers being bundled into a car by strangers, watching the world blur by through rain-soaked windows as she was taken to the orphanage. She remembers the cold, impersonal rooms of the place, the way the other children looked at her like she was something strange, something broken. But most of all, she remembers the stories her mother told her before it all fell apart.

Her mother's voice was always soothing, always full of life, even in the moments when Emma sensed that things weren't quite right. The stories were their shared secret, a way to escape the heaviness that seemed to press down on their little family. Now, standing in this strange, impossible library,

Emma wonders if those stories were more than just escapes. Her mother was trying to prepare her for something like this.

But why? Why would her mother know about this place? And what did it have to do with Emma's past?

A flash of movement catches Emma's eye, pulling her from her thoughts. Up ahead, where the rows of shelves break into another clearing, she sees a figure dart between the shadows. Unlike the older version of herself from earlier, this figure is small, almost childlike, and it moves with a quick, nervous energy.

"Hey!" Emma calls out, her voice breaking the heavy silence. She breaks into a run, her feet pounding against the floor as she chases after the figure. "Wait!"

The figure doesn't stop disappearing around a corner of shelves. Emma races after it, her ragged shoes slapping against the cold stone floor. Her heart thunders in her chest, the air sharp in her lungs, but she keeps going, her instincts driving her forward.

She turns the corner, skidding to a halt as she finds herself in a new section of the library—one that feels different from the rest. The air here is colder, the light dimmer. The shelves are narrower, more cramped, and the books that line them are older, more fragile, their spines cracked and yellowed with age.

And standing in the middle of it all, staring right at her, is the figure.

It's a girl, no older than Emma, but there's something strange about her; something not right. Her eyes are wide and glassy, her skin pale, almost translucent. Her clothes, a faded dress that might have once been white, hang loosely on her thin frame, and her hair is tangled and wild, like she's been running for a very long time.

Emma takes a cautious step forward. "Who are you?"

The girl doesn't respond. She just stands there, staring at Emma with those wide, unblinking eyes. For a moment, Emma wonders if the girl is even real, or if she's just another trick of the library, another piece of the puzzle designed to confuse her.

"I... I'm trying to find a way out," Emma says, her voice softer now. "Do you know how to get out of here?"

The girl tilts her head slightly, her expression still blank, but there's something in her eyes— something sad, almost lost. Slowly, she lifts a hand

and points to a book on the nearest shelf. Emma follows her gaze, her heart pounding as she steps closer to the shelf.

The book the girl is pointing to is small and plain, its cover a deep, weathered brown. Unlike the other books she's seen in the library, this one looks unassuming, almost forgettable. But as Emma reaches for it, she feels that strange pull again; the same pull that led her to the library in the first place.

Her fingers close around the spine of the book, and the moment she pulls it free from the shelf, the air around her seems to shift. The girl takes a step back, her eyes never leaving Emma, and for the first time, Emma hears her speak.

"You can't leave," the girl says, her voice barely a whisper. "Not until you remember."

Emma's blood runs cold. "What do you mean? Remember what?"

The girl doesn't answer. Instead, she fades away, dissolving into the shadows like mist. Emma is left standing alone in the narrow aisle, the book in her hands and the weight of the girl's words pressing down on her chest.

*Not until you remember.*

Emma's heart pounds as she stares down at the book. Her hands shake slightly as she opens it, half-expecting the pages to be blank like so many others she's seen. But they're not. The pages are filled with words, written in neat, flowing script. And as Emma reads the first few lines, her breath catches in her throat.

It's her mother's story. The story her mother used to tell her every night before bed—the one about a girl who could travel between worlds. The one Emma thought was just a fairy tale. But here it is, written in black and white, as if the library itself has pulled it from Emma's memory and placed it in this book.

*The key to her memory.*

Emma turns the pages, her eyes scanning the familiar words. But as she reads, something strange begins to happen. The story changes. The words shift and blur, new lines appearing on the page that Emma has never heard before. The girl in the story, the girl who travels between worlds, is not just a character anymore. She's real. She's Emma.

Emma's hands tremble as the truth begins to sink in. The story her mother told her, it wasn't just a bedtime tale. It was a clue, a map, a way for Emma to understand who she really is. She's the girl in the story. The library, the worlds inside the books, the creatures, the puzzles; it's all connected to her.

But why? Why would her mother tell her this story? Did her mother know Emma would end up here? And what does it all mean?

Suddenly, the pages of the book begin to glow, and the air around Emma shifts again. The library seems to ripple, the shelves blurring and twisting as if the entire building is coming alive. Emma stumbles back, clutching the book to her chest as the ground beneath her feet begins to tremble.

The whisper returns, louder now, echoing through the library like a distant voice continued the wind.

*"Return... before dawn..."*

Panic rises in Emma's chest. Time is running out. She has to find a way out of here before it's too late. But she can't leave; not until she remembers.

*Not until you understand.*

The book in her hands glows brighter, and Emma feels a strange warmth spread through her chest. The pull is stronger now, more insistent, like it's leading her toward something important.

Without thinking, Emma turns and starts running. She doesn't know where she's going, but the pull in her chest guides her, tugging her toward the heart of the library. The shelves blur past her as she runs, the floor vibrating beneath her feet as the library shifts and changes around her.

She races through the endless aisles, her breath coming in quick, shallow gasps. The whisper grows louder, filling the air, pressing down on her.

*"Return before dawn..."*

Emma's legs burn, but she doesn't stop. She can't. The pull in her chest is stronger than ever, and she knows, somehow, that she's getting closer to the answer. Closer to the truth.

She rounds a corner, skidding to a halt as she finds herself in front of a massive, ornate door. It's unlike any door she's seen in the library before; tall and imposing, with intricate carvings that seem to shimmer in the dim light. And in the center of the door, etched in gold, is a symbol.

*A key.*

Emma's heart races as she steps closer, her fingers trembling as she reaches for the handle. The door is warm to the touch, and as she grasps the handle, the pull in her chest becomes almost unbearable.

She knows what this is. This is the door for which she's been searching. The door to the past. The door that holds the key to everything.

With a deep breath, Emma pulls the door open.

Light floods the room, and for a moment, Emma is blind. But as her eyes adjust, she steps through the door and into a world she never expected.

The past. *Her past*.

And standing in the middle of it all, waiting for her, is the truth she's been running from her whole life.

Emma takes a deep breath, her heart pounding in her chest.

# Chapter 5: Into the Depths

The moment Emma steps through the door, the air changes. The scent of saltwater and sea-weed fills her lungs, and the low rumble of distant waves crashes in her ears. She blinks, her eyes adjusting to the bright light of day, so different from the dim, shadowy library she's just left behind.

The world around her is vast and untamed. She stands on the deck of a massive ship, its weathered wooden boards creaking beneath her feet. The sails above her billow in the wind, catching the sunlight as they stretch toward the sky. The horizon is endless, a deep blue ocean stretching out in every direction, its waves glistening like jewels under the sun.

For a moment, Emma could only stand there, her breath caught in her throat. She's been in strange worlds before, but this feels different. The salty wind stings her cheeks, and the cold spray of the sea touches her skin. It's all so real.

On the pirate ship, Emma looks down and notices she is dressed in a simple, worn tunic made of rough brown linen, belted loosely at the waist with a piece of frayed rope. Over it, she is wearing a weathered coat, too large for her small frame, with its sleeves rolled up unevenly to her elbows. Her pants, torn and patched in several places, clinging to her legs, tucked into boots that have seen better days, the leather scuffed and cracked. Her once-blonde hair, now a tangled mess of scraggly waves, falls around her face in uneven lengths, dirt and saltwater making it appear darker than it is. Her pale skin is smudged with grime, and her sharp blue eyes, though tired, gleam with determination and a spark of adventure, showing the strength and resilience that have kept her going through her journey. Despite the roughness of her appearance, there's a fierce beauty about her.

The moment Emma steps forward, the ship lurches violently, throwing her out of balance. She stumbles, grabbing the edge of the railing for support as the ship sways beneath her. Shouts fill the air, men and women scrambling across the deck as the ship struggles against the rolling waves.

It's then that she sees them, pirates.

They rush about, pulling ropes, tying knots, their faces hardened by the sea and sun. Their clothes are ragged, like her own, but there's a fierce determination in their eyes. They work with the kind of precision that only comes from years of surviving the open sea. Their voices are rough, barking orders at each other as they fight to keep the ship steady.

And then, above it all, a voice cuts through the chaos; strong, commanding, and oddly familiar.

"Hold steady, you scurvy lot! We won't be taken down by a little storm!"

Emma's eyes are drawn to the figure at the helm; a woman standing tall, her hands gripping the ship's wheel.

The captain of the pirate ship is a striking figure, tall and commanding, with an air of authority that leaves no room for doubt. She wears a long, tattered coat of deep crimson, the once-vibrant fabric now faded by the salt and sun, but still regal in its own weathered way.

The coat is adorned with brass buttons, dulled with age, and its hem trails behind her as she strides across the deck. A wide-brimmed hat, tipped low over her face, casts a shadow over her sharp, sun-kissed features, but doesn't hide the fierce intelligence in her stormy gray eyes. Her hair, long and black, streaked with silver from years at sea, is pulled back into a loose knot, though strands of it whip free in the wind. Around her neck, she wears a leather strap bearing a tarnished compass that rarely leaves her side, and a cutlass hangs from her hip, its hilt worn from countless battles. Her boots, high and laced, are caked with mud and sand from distant shores, giving her the look of someone who has traveled far, and faced many dangers,  hardened by the life of living out on the sea.

For a moment, Emma can't move, her heart is racing in her chest. There's something about the captain; something that stirs a memory deep inside her, a flicker of recognition. But before she can figure it out, the captain's gaze locks onto her.

"You there!" the captain shouts, her voice sharp and commanding. "What are you standing around for? Get to work, or you'll be swimming with the sharks!"

Emma opens her mouth to respond, but the words stick in her throat.

The captain strides across the deck toward her, her coat flaring behind her as she moves with a confidence that leaves Emma feeling small and out of place. The captain's eyes narrow as she looks Emma up and down, her gaze lingering on Emma's ragged clothes and dirt-smudged face.

"Who are ye?" the captain asks, her voice lower now, more curious than accusing. "Ye don't look like one of my crew."

Emma swallows hard, her mind racing for an answer. "I... I'm Emma," she stammers, gripping the railing tightly. "I didn't mean to be here. I just.."

Before she can finish, the ship lurches again, and the wind picks up, howling through the sails. The captain lets out a string of curses under her breath, grabbing the wheel and steering the ship back on course. The crew scrambles around them, but Emma feels like the whole world has narrowed down to just her and the captain.

"Ye are no pirate, that be sure," the captain says, her voice a mix of suspicion and curiosity. "So, what are ye doing on my ship, land lover?"

Emma hesitates. She can't explain everything, not now, not when the ship is barely holding together, and a storm is brewing on the horizon. But she feels that she pulls again; the one that's been guiding her ever since she stepped into the library. There's something about this place, something important she's meant to discover.

"I... I'm looking for something," Emma says, her voice barely audible over the wind and waves. "Something important."

The captain raises an eyebrow. "Argh, aren't we all, girl."

Before Emma can ask what she means, the captain turns her attention back to the ship, barking orders at the crew. The wind howls, and the ship tilts precariously as the waves grow taller, crashing against the sides of the vessel with a deafening roar. Emma holds on to the railing, her knuckles white as the storm closes in around them.

For a moment, all she can think about is surviving. The wind tears at her clothes, the rain stings her skin, and the sea roars beneath her like a living thing. But then, something strange happens.

As the storm rages, Emma feels a warmth spread through her chest. It's faint at first, like a flicker of candlelight, but it grows stronger, brighter, until it feels like a beacon inside her. She glances down at her hands, and there a faint but unmistakable glow of the key symbol from the book. It's pulsing in time with her heartbeat, a reminder that she's not just here by chance. There's something she's meant to find, something tied to the puzzle of the library and her mother's story.

*The key to memory,* Emma thinks, her heart pounding. But what does it mean? What is she supposed to remember?

As if in answer, a flash of memory surges through her mother's voice, soft and full of wonder as she told the story of the girl who could travel between worlds. Emma can almost hear her now, feel the warmth of her mother's arms around her as she listened, wide-eyed, to the tales of adventure and magic.

But there was more to the story, something Emma had forgotten. Something about a pirate ship, lost to time and cursed by the sea. A ship that carried a treasure more valuable than gold.

Her mother's voice echoes in her mind: *"The ship sails endlessly, lost between worlds. And only the one who remembers the past can set it free."*

Emma's breath catches in her throat. This is it. The ship from her mother's story, it's real. And she's standing on it.

The storm seems to intensify, the waves crashing harder against the ship as if the sea itself is trying to stop her from realizing the truth. But Emma won't be deterred. She steps forward, her eyes locking onto the captain, who is now fighting to keep the ship from capsizing.

"I know this ship!" Emma shouts over the roar of the wind. "I know what it's looking for!"

The captain turns, her eyes narrowing. "What are ye talking about, land lover?"

"This ship. It's cursed," Emma says, the words tumbling out of her. "It's been lost between worlds, trapped by the sea. There's a treasure, but it's not gold. It's something else, something tied to memories."

The captain's eyes widen, but before she can respond, the ship lurches violently, and a massive wave crashes over the deck, sweeping Emma off her feet. She tumbles across the slick wooden boards, gasping for breath as the cold sea water drenches her clothes.

A hand grabs her arm, pulling her up. Emma blinks through the rain, and there, standing before her, is the captain—her eyes filled with a mixture of disbelief and something else... something like hope.

"Ye can't be serious," the captain says, her voice low. "Ye actually know about this here curse."

Emma nods, still catching her breath. "I think I do. My mother... she used to tell me stories about this ship. She knew."

The captain stares at her for a long moment, the storm raging around them. And then, slowly, she releases Emma's arm and steps back, her expression hardening.

"If ye know the truth," the captain says, "then ye know what needs to be done, argh."

"I have to find it," Emma says. "The memory. It's the only way to break the curse."

The captain nods grimly. "Then we'd better survive this here storm. We're close that island. If ye are right... we'll find what we're looking for yonder."

The ship creaks and groans beneath them, but there's a sense of purpose now, a direction. Emma stands beside the captain, her heart pounding with fear and determination. She doesn't have all the answers yet, but she knows this is part of the puzzle. And whatever lies ahead, she'll face it.

As the storm howls and the ship sails toward the island, Emma feels her mother's presence, like a whisper in the wind. There are more memories to uncover, more secrets to reveal. And she won't stop until she finds them all.

# Chapter 6: The Cursed Isle

The wind howled in Emma's ears, saltwater stinging her skin as the storm raged around the ship. Waves crashed against the hull, and the deck tilted beneath her feet, but Emma gripped the railing with white-knuckled determination. She had never been on a ship before, much less in the middle of a storm. But there was something about the sea that felt oddly familiar, like a part of her story that had been waiting to unfold.

Beside her, the captain, a fearsome woman with wild hair and a permanent scowl, stood tall, hands gripping the wheel like she was wrestling with the storm itself. The island was looming closer now, barely visible through the sheets of rain, but Emma felt its pull in her chest, growing stronger with every wave.

"What do ye know about this curse, girl?" the captain barked over the wind. Her eyes narrowed at Emma with suspicion, and something else, like fear. "Why is me ship lost? Why are we cursed to sail these bloody waters?"

Emma opened her mouth to respond, but it was hard to concentrate with the storm roaring in her ears. She hesitated, fumbling for words. "Well... it's not exactly about treasure. Not the kind you're used to, anyway."

The captain squinted at her. "Not treasure?" She let out a gruff laugh, which quickly turned into a cough as seawater splashed into her mouth. "What's a curse got to do with anything else then, argh?"

Emma flinched as a wave crashed over the deck. "You've lost time," she shouted, her voice shaking but growing stronger. "You and your crew... you've been sailing in circles, caught between worlds, between stories, and you don't even remember how it happened!"

The captain's face twisted into a grimace, and she squinted suspiciously at Emma. "And ye reckon ye know this, why?"

Emma swallowed hard. "My mother. She told me stories about a ship cursed by the sea. She knew about this place... and about you."

The captain's grip on the wheel tightened so hard that her knuckles turned white. She opened her mouth to say something, but another wave hit the side of the ship, sending both of them stumbling. Emma caught herself on the railing, but the captain just growled, muttering curses under her breath.

Suddenly, a fish flopped out of nowhere and slapped the captain squarely in the face.

Emma gasped; eyes wide in shock. But instead of getting angry, the captain just stood there, blinking water, and wiping it off her face in disbelief. "Well, that's just insult to injury, innit?"

Emma bit her lip, trying not to laugh. The captain wiped the fish slime off her cheek and tossed the fish back into the sea with a sour look. "Right," she grumbled, "let's get to that blasted island before I'm slapped by a squid."

The ship creaked and groaned as it drew closer to the jagged shoreline. The island loomed ahead, dark and foreboding. The crew scrambled to lower the anchor, their eyes darting nervously between the waves and Emma, as if they weren't sure who or what to fear more.

Emma and the captain descended onto the rocky beach. Rain lashed at their faces, and the wind whipped at their clothes, but Emma couldn't shake the feeling that this place, this cursed island, held the answers she had been searching for.

The captain scowled at her as they trudged inland. "I've sailed through storms worse than this," she muttered, "but I ain't never had to deal with a fish attack before."

Emma stifled a snort. "Maybe it was cursed too."

The captain shot her a sideways glance, one eyebrow raised. "Ye think a fish got its own curse, eh? Poor devil."

As they moved deeper into the island, the trees twisted like crooked fingers, their branches reaching out as if trying to pull them into the darkness. The path narrowed, and the air grew colder, filled with an eerie silence. Emma felt the weight of the island pressing down on her, thick like fog.

Suddenly, a loud squawk echoed through the trees. Both Emma and the captain froze as a large, bedraggled parrot flew out of nowhere and landed on a branch, glaring at them with beady eyes.

"Who goes there?!" the parrot screeched, hopping from one foot to the other. "State your business, ya landlubbers!"

Emma blinked, taken aback. "Um... we're here to break the curse?"

The parrot tilted its head, eyeing them suspiciously. "Curse, eh? Don't know nothin' about no curse. Just here for the snacks!"

The captain rolled her eyes. "Great. Even the birds here are pirates."

The parrot fluffed its feathers indignantly. "I'm a respectable seagull, thank you very much!"

Emma blinked. "You're a parrot."

"Details!" the parrot squawked. "Now, where's me crackers?"

The captain waved the bird away, grumbling under her breath. "Out of me way, featherbrain, we've got a curse to break."

They continued on, leaving the indignant parrot behind. Soon, the entrance to a cave loomed ahead, it was dark and damp inside. The captain eyed it warily, her earlier bravado seeming to waver. "This the place, then?"

Emma nodded, her heart pounding. "This is where we'll find the memories."

The captain stepped forward, scowling into the cave's mouth. "Let's get this over with."

Inside, the air was thick and hot, and the sound of dripping water echoed through the darkness. They pressed forward until they reached the back of the cave, where a shimmering pool of water glowed faintly in the darkness.

"That's it," Emma whispered, her voice trembling. "That's where the memories are."

The captain stepped forward cautiously, glancing at the pool. "So, what? We jump in and suddenly remember we left the stove on?"

Emma sighed. "Not exactly..."

But before she could explain, the captain had already stepped into the pool with a loud splash. Emma cringed, waiting for something dramatic to happen, but all that came was a low, haunting hum, followed by the captain shouting, "Argh, it's freezing!"

The pool began to ripple, and memories rose to the surface like bubbles, swirling around them in a misty fog. As they watched, Emma saw flashes of the past; fragments of the crew's lives, their lost time, and then, her mother. Her mother's face appeared in the mist, her eyes full of sadness and wisdom.

Emma gasped; her chest tight with emotion. The captain, meanwhile, stared at the visions, her jaw slack. "Well, I'll be," she muttered. "Ye weren't lying."

Emma turned to her, heart racing. "This is it. This is how we break the curse."

The captain nodded, her face pale. "Right then. Let's finish this before fish be slapping me again ."

## Chapter 7: The Dragon's Puzzle

The water feels colder than Emma expects as it rises around her legs, sending a shiver through her body. She stands shoulder to shoulder with the captain, both of them peering into the shimmering depths of the pool. The surface ripples, distorting the reflections of their faces, but Emma can sense that something is about to change, something deep and important, tied to the ship, to her mother, and to whatever comes next.

Her breath catches as the water begins to glow more brightly, illuminating the entire cave with an ethereal light. And then the memories rise. They surge out of the water, twisting and coiling like tendrils of mist, forming scenes that flicker and shift before her eyes.

At first, Emma sees the captain's memories. Images flash quickly: the ship in its prime, sails full of wind as it cuts through the ocean; the captain standing proudly at the helm, her eyes sharp and filled with purpose. But then, the memory twists as darkness falls, and a strange fog envelops the ship. Figures in shadowy cloaks appear on the deck, murmuring words that Emma can't understand. The crew collapses one by one, as if pulled into a deep sleep. And then everything fades into blackness, leaving only the sound of the waves crashing against the cursed ship.

The captain gasps beside her, her hands trembling. "So that's how it happened," she whispers. "Someone cursed us, something, out there in the fog. I couldn't save me crew or me ship."

Emma's chest tightens. This is why they've been sailing in circles, lost in time and memory. But it's not just the ship's curse. There's more, something connected to her, to her own past.

As if responding to her thoughts, the memories shift again, this time pulling Emma into them. She watches, wide-eyed, as images of her mother flicker to life before her. Her mother stands in their small, cozy home, holding a book in her hands, the very same one Emma has carried in her pocket since she entered the library. Her mother's voice is gentle, warm, and familiar.

"Remember, Emma," her mother says, her face soft but serious. "There are worlds inside every book, and not all of them are safe. But you must always trust yourself and your memories. They will guide you, even when things seem impossible."

The image shifts, and now her mother is sitting on the edge of Emma's bed, telling her the story of a dragon, one that guards a mountain of memories, a dragon that holds the key to unlocking the past. Emma remembers this story, one of the last her mother told her before she was gone.

But there's something different about the way her mother says it now. In the memory, her mother looks directly at Emma, her eyes full of meaning. "When the time comes, you'll need to face the dragon. It will be hard, but the memories it guards are the most important ones of all."

The vision dissolves, and Emma's heart pounds in her chest and the sound of it rings in her ears. The dragon, the one from her mother's story; it's real. And it holds the next piece of the puzzle. But what does the dragon guard? What memories could be so dangerous that they need a guardian like that?

The water ripples again, and for a moment, the cave seems to shimmer with the promise of something more. Emma feels the pull even stronger now, more urgent. She knows what she has to do.

"The dragon," she whispers, her voice barely audible. "It's the next step. I have to face it."

The captain looks at her, confusion flickering across her face. "A dragon? What are ye talking about land lover, ain't that nothing but fairy tales?"

"My mother told me about it," Emma explains, her heart racing as she pieces it all together. "It's guarding something, memories that were taken. The curse on your ship, it's part of this, but so is my past. I need to find those memories."

The captain frowns, she gazes intensely. "And how exactly do ye plan to find this here dragon?"

Emma closes her eyes, letting the memory of her mother's voice guide her. "There's another book," she says, her voice steady despite the fear creeping into her chest. "Somewhere in the library. I have to jump into that story, into the world where the dragon lives."

Before the captain can respond, the cave around them begins to shift. The walls ripple like water, and the ground beneath their feet seems to tremble. Emma gasps, feeling the pull intensify as if the library itself is calling her back. She looks down at the glowing pool, its surface swirling with memories, and knows that her time here is coming to an end.

"I have to go," she says, her voice urgent. "The library's pulling me back."

The captain grabs her arm, her grip firm. "Wait! What happens to me crew and ship?"

Emma meets the captain's eyes, her own filled with determination. "You have to remember like I did. That's the only way to break the curse. When you find it, when you truly remember, you'll be free."

The captain nods, her expression grim but hopeful. "I'll find it, land lover. Argh, that be sure."

Emma nods, her heart pounding in her chest as the cave dissolves around her. The captain's face fades into the mist, and suddenly, she's falling, falling back into the endless expanse of the library.

The familiar scent of old books fills her nose, and when Emma opens her eyes, she's back in the heart of the library, standing between towering shelves of ancient tomes. Her clothes are still damp from the pool, and her heart races as she catches her breath, the weight of what she's just learned pressing down on her. Emma begins to feel tired; time is pressing on.

But there's no time to rest. The pull is still there, drawing her deeper into the library's labyrinth. She moves quickly, scanning the shelves for the book she needs, the one that holds the dragon's world.

After what feels like an eternity, she finds it.

The book is massive, bound in dark leather with a shimmering emblem of a dragon on the cover. Emma's fingers tremble as she pulls them free from the shelf. The title is simple and clear: *The Mountain of Memories.*

"This is it," Emma whispers to herself, her pulse quickening. She knows the dragon lies within these pages, waiting for her. And with it, the key to unlocking more of her lost memories that could explain everything.

Without hesitating, Emma opens the book.

The world shifts around her, and once again, she's pulled inside.

Emma lands with a soft thud on the rocky ground, the air cool and crisp around her. She's on the mountainside, the jagged cliffs rising high above her, and in the distance, she hears the low, rumbling growl of something massive. Her heart skips a beat as she looks up at the towering peak, shrouded in mist. The dragon is up there, waiting.

The wind whips through her hair, carrying the scent of smoke and something ancient, something powerful.

The climb is steep, the path treacherous. Rocks shift beneath her feet, and more than once, Emma stumbles, catching herself on jagged edges as she makes her way higher up the mountain. Her heart pounds in her chest, fear gnawing at the edges of her resolve, but she refuses to turn back. She's come too far.

As she climbs, fragments of her mother's voice echo in her mind, pieces of the story she now knows to be real.

"The dragon guards the past," her mother had said. "But the past isn't always easy to face."

The past. That's what she's here for, the memories she's lost, the pieces of herself that have been taken. She can feel it in her bones now, a certainty growing stronger with every step.

At last, she reaches the top of the mountain. The peak is a wide, flat plateau, and in the center, curled around a massive pile of shimmering stones, lies the dragon.

Its scales gleam in the pale light, a deep emerald green that shifts to black as it moves. Its eyes, the color of molten gold, snap open the moment Emma steps onto the plateau. The dragon raises its head, smoke curling from its nostrils as it watches her with an intensity that makes her stomach twist.

For a long moment, neither of them moves.

Then the dragon speaks, its voice a low, rumbling growl that shakes the very ground beneath her feet.

"I have been waiting for you Emma. So, you've come for what was taken."

Emma nods, her throat tight. "Yes. I need the memories you guard."

The dragon's eyes narrow, and it body shifts slightly, its massive tail curling around a pile of stones. "Memories are not given freely. They must be earned."

Emma takes a deep breath, her heart pounding in her chest. "What do I have to do?"

The dragon lowers its head,  it blinks its golden eyes that are gleaming. "You must face what you fear most. Only then will the memories be yours."

Emma's hands tremble, but she stands tall, her gaze locked with the dragon's. She knows what's coming, and she knows it won't be easy.

The ground shifts beneath her, and suddenly, the past rises up to meet her.

Emma's heart races as the memories flood in, images of her mother, the library, and the truth she's been avoiding for so long.

# Chapter 8: The Battle Within

"I'm not afraid," she whispers, though the words sound hollow in the face of this massive creature. The truth is, she's terrified. Not of the dragon, but of what it's about to show her.

As she stands there, the ground beneath her feet begins to shift. The rocky plateau wavers, melting away into mist. Emma gasps as the air around her turns dark and cold, the dragon fading into the distance. She is no longer on the mountaintop. The world around her twists, reshaping itself into something familiar and terrifying all at once.

She's back at the orphanage.

The once-large and bustling place looms over her now, its walls darker and more ominous than she remembers. The smell of old wood and dust fills her nose, and the faint echo of children's laughter drifts through the corridors. But the laughter is cold, eerie, like ghosts from her past haunting the halls.

Emma freezes in place, her chest tightening. This is where she grew up, where she spent years feeling lost and unwanted. The orphanage, where no one came for her, no one looked for her, where she learned that she was truly alone. This is her greatest fear. Not monsters, not dragons, but the crushing loneliness that she has carried with her for as long as she can remember.

The mist thickens around her, and suddenly she's no longer standing in the empty hallway of the orphanage. She's in her old room, a small, dimly lit space with a single bed pressed up against the wall. The room looks just as it did the day she left: the frayed quilt on the bed, the chipped paint on the windowsill, and the tiny, worn-out bookshelf where she kept the few books she had. Books that were her only escape from this place.

Her younger self sits on the bed, staring out the window, waiting, always waiting. For someone to come for her. For a family. For the place where she belonged. But no one has ever come for her.

Emma's breath catches in her throat as she watches the scene unfold. The loneliness, the sadness, it all comes rushing back, flooding her chest with a familiar ache. She wants to reach out to the girl on the bed, to tell her that it's going to be okay, that one day she'll find a way out of this place. But the younger Emma doesn't move. She just stares at the door, waiting.

"You can't save her," a voice whispers in the darkness, cold and harsh. "You can't change what's already happened."

Emma turns, her pulse quickening. Standing in the doorway is a figure cloaked in shadow, its features hidden. But Emma knows who it is, it's the part of herself she's been running from. The part that tells her she's alone, that no matter how many worlds she jumps into, how many memories she unlocks, the loneliness will always be there, lurking in the corners of her heart.

"You're always going to be alone," the shadow says, stepping closer. "No one will ever come for you. Not then, not now."

Emma's chest constricts, the words cut her deep. This is her greatest fear, the fear that no matter what she does, no matter how far she runs, she'll never escape the feeling of being unwanted. That she'll always be the girl sitting alone on the bed, waiting for someone who will never come.

Tears prick the corners of her eyes, but Emma forces herself to stand tall, to face the shadow.

She's not that girl anymore. She's faced monsters, dragons, and curses, and she's still standing.

"You're wrong," Emma says, her voice shaking but stronger than before. "I'm not alone. I've fought too hard, come too far, to let you control me."

The shadow laughs, cold and cruel. "You think you're strong enough to fight me? To fight the truth?"

"Yes," Emma says, her fists clenching. "Because I'm not just that scared little girl anymore. I've changed. I've found courage, and I'm not waiting for someone to save me; I'm saving myself."

The shadow shifts, its form flickering as if uncertain. The mist around them grows thinner, and Emma feels the weight on her chest begins to lift. She takes a deep breath, steadying herself, refusing to let the fear win.

"I may be afraid," Emma says, her voice firm, "but I won't let it stop me. Not anymore."

The shadow lets out a low hiss, but it's fading, dissolving into the mist that surrounds them. The younger version of Emma disappears as well, and the orphanage, with all its cold memories, begins to fade.

The dragon's voice echoes in the distance. "You've faced your fear."

The mist lifts, and Emma is back on the mountaintop, the dragon still coiled around its shimmering hoard. But something is different now. The weight in her chest has lifted, the ache of loneliness still there but not as crushing, not as powerful as it was before.

The dragon watches her with those golden eyes, its expression unreadable.

"You've earned the memories," it says, its voice low and rumbling. "But there is still more to face. More to unlock."

Emma nods, her chest rising and falling with steady breaths. She feels stronger now, surer of herself, but she knows the journey isn't over. The memories may help her unlock the next puzzle, but she has to keep moving forward.

The dragon shifts, revealing something beneath its massive tail, a key. It's not just any key, though. It glows with an eerie light, pulsing softly as if it's alive. Emma steps forward, her hand reaching for it. As her fingers close around the key, she feels a surge of warmth spread through her, filling her with a sense of purpose.

"The next step awaits," the dragon says, its voice fading as the world around Emma begins to shimmer and blur. "Face the ghost of your past."

---

The pirate crew, who had been cursed to sail endlessly, slowly transformed because of Emma's bravery. Their once hollow, forgetful eyes brightened with recognition, and their faces softened with relief. The weight of the curse lifted. The years they had lost came flooding back to them.

The captain's fierce scowl was replaced by something almost tender as she looked at her crew, whole and free for the first time in what felt like centuries.

The ship, no longer bound by magic, would sail once more, but this time, with a purpose. They would return home, to the lives they had long forgotten, their ties to the cursed island and its haunted waters finally severed.

The captain raises her glass in Emma's honor, "thanks to the land lover, for setting us free!"

Emma returns to the library, the book she holds is dull. She moves quickly across many titles until she sees the glow of another book.

Touching it, in a flash of light she falls through into another world once more.

When Emma opens her eyes, she finds herself standing in front of a grand, crumbling mansion. The air is thick with fog, and the trees surrounding the mansion are twisted and gnarled, their branches reaching toward the sky like skeletal fingers trying to snatch the moon. The mansion itself looms before her, its windows are dark and empty, the doors slightly ajar as if beckoning her to come in.

The key in her hand pulses, and Emma knows this is the next puzzle, the next book she's jumped into.

Taking a deep breath, Emma steps toward the mansion, her thin shoes crunching on the gravel path. The closer she gets, the more she can feel the presence of someone watching her.

The mansion creaks as she pushes the door open, revealing a dark, empty foyer. Cobwebs drape the chandeliers, and the furniture is covered with blankets and are in thick layers of dust. The silence is not comforting, broken only by the faint sound of footsteps echoing from somewhere deep within the mansion.

Emma's heart pounds, gripping the key tightly in her hand.

A voice echoes through the halls, low and haunting. "Who dares enter my domain?"

Emma swallows hard, her pulse quickening. "I'm here to unlock the past," she says, her voice steady despite the fear bubbling inside her. "I'm here for memories that you can show me."

The voice chuckles, cold and eerie. "Then you must solve the riddle of the dead."

Emma steps into the darkness, her heart racing as the mansion closes in around her.

The floor creaks behind her. Emma spins around, her heart leaping into her throat. The mansion's heavy silence presses down on her, but no one is there. Only the shadows stretch across the room, playing tricks in her eyes.

"Show yourself!" Emma shouts, her voice defiant despite the fear swirling around in her stomach, making her feel nauseous.

For a moment, nothing happens. Then, from the far end of the room, a figure emerges from the shadows. A Tall and translucent cloaked in dark robes figure appears, its face hidden beneath a wide-brimmed hat. It glides toward her without making a sound, and as it approaches, the air grows colder, biting into her skin.

Emma stands her ground, clutching the key as if it's the only thing tethering her to this world.

The figure stops just a few feet from her, its form flickering like the light of a dying candle. And when it speaks, its voice is low, filled with a weariness that seeps into Emma's bones.

"I was once like you," it says, its voice barely above a whisper. "Alive. Searching for answers. But now, I am bound to this place."

Emma swallows hard. "Who are you?"

The figure hesitates, as if struggling to remember. "I am... or was... the detective. I was sent here long ago to solve the mystery of this mansion. But it was not just a house of stone and wood, it was a prison. A place where secrets festered, and here, where the past never truly dies."

Emma's mind races. She remembers her mother's Halloween story, the one about a ghost detective trapped in a haunted mansion, doomed to walk its halls for eternity. But she never imagined it was real; never thought she'd stand here.

"What happened here?" Emma asks, her voice trembling despite her efforts to sound brave.

The ghost's hollow eyes meet hers, and for a moment, Emma feels a wave of sorrow wash over her, an overwhelming sense of loss and regret.

"The mansion," the ghost detective says slowly, "is cursed by the memories of those who lived and died within its walls. They cannot rest. Their secrets, their betrayals, their sin, are all tied to this place. The living and the dead are bound together, forever. Memories of living in the past is the fate of those who do not move forward in life."

The detective's form flickers again, as if struggling to remain solid. Emma can feel the weight of the mansion bearing down on her, the oppressive energy of the souls trapped here.

"I need those memories," Emma says, her voice firmer now. "I just need them.."

The detective watches her, its hollow gaze unreadable. Then, it gestures toward the grand staircase. "The memories you seek are not in the light. They are buried in the darkness."

Taking a deep breath, Emma steps toward the staircase. The detective's form fades into the shadows once more, leaving her alone in the heavy silence of the house.

The stairs groan under her weight as she ascends, her every step sending echoes through the vast, empty hall. The colder the air gets, the higher she climbs. By the time she reaches the landing, it feels as though she's stepped into a tomb.

A long corridor stretches out before her, lined with closed doors. Emma can't shake the feeling that something is waiting for her behind one of them, something that has been waiting for a long, long time.

She walks slowly down the corridor, brushing her hand against the walls, feeling the cool, damp stone beneath her fingers. As she passes each door, she hears faint whispers, like voices trapped behind the wood, murmuring secrets she can't quite make out.

But it's the door at the end of the hall that draws her in. Unlike the others, this one is slightly darker, and from within, a faint light flickers, casting eerie shadows onto the floor.

Emma's pulse quickens as she steps closer, her heart racing with both fear and anticipation. She pushes the door open, and the room beyond is bathed in a soft, golden glow.

It's a study, filled with towering bookshelves and a large desk in the center. Papers are scattered across the desk, and an old oil lamp flickers on its surface, casting long shadows on the walls.

But it's the figure standing at the desk that makes Emma's breath catch in her throat.

It's her mother.

At least, it looks like her mother. The figure is turned away from Emma, bent over the desk as though searching for something, her hair falling in soft waves around her shoulders, just like Emma remembers.

"Mom?" Emma whispers, her voice trembling.

The figure doesn't move.

Emma's feet feel heavy, as though they're rooted to the floor, but she forces herself to step into the room, her heart pounding in her chest. She wants to run to her, to hold her mother in her arms, but something about the scene feels wrong. There's a stillness in the air, a tension that makes her hesitate.

"Mom?" she says again, louder this time.

Slowly, the figure turns, and Emma's heart sinks.

It's not her mother.

The figure's face is pale, its eyes hollow and empty. The resemblance is there, the same shape of her face, the same softness in her features, but this is a ghost, a memory twisted by time and the curse of the mansion.

Emma feels a lump form in her throat, the weight of her grief threatening to overwhelm her. But she doesn't run. She knows now what this is.

It's not her mother. It's a test, a final challenge before she can unlock the next piece of the puzzle.

"I miss you," Emma whispers, tears stinging her eyes. "But you're not real. You're not really here."

The ghost tilts its head, watching her with those empty, hollow eyes. And then it speaks, its voice soft and distant, like an echo from another time.

"You must let go of the past, Emma," the ghost says. "Your father and I died long ago; we cannot come for you as you wish. I am so sorry that no one ever told you."

Emma's heart feels the pain of sorrow that has been aching for many years. She knows the ghost is right. She has to let go of the grief, of the loneliness, of the fear that she was abandoned by her parents. But it's so hard. Harder than any battle she's faced before.

With trembling hands, Emma raises the glowing key, holding it in front of her. "I'm ready," she says, her voice shaking. "I'm ready to let go. But I wanted to always tell you, before you left, I love you and I won't forget you, not ever."

The ghost's form flickers, and for a moment, Emma swears she sees a flicker of warmth in its hollow eyes, like her mother's love shining through the darkness. "We love you too, sweetness."

And then the ghost disappears.

The room goes quiet, and the key in Emma's hand glows brighter, pulsing with a soft, steady rhythm. She knows now that she's unlocked something important; not just the memories, but a part of herself she's been holding onto for too long.

The room fades around her, the walls of the mansion dissolving into mist, and Emma feels the familiar pull of the library drawing her back. She closes her eyes, letting the warmth of the key guide her.

When she opens them again, she's standing in the library once more, the towering shelves stretching out before her.

But something is different now. She feels lighter, freer, as though she's shed a burden she's carried for too long.

# Chapter 9: The Pharaoh's Riddle

The library's shelves seem to stretch forever, towering above Emma like the walls of a great maze. The soft flicker of candlelight and the scent of ancient parchment fill the air. She's been through, Emma feels an odd comfort in this place, but she knows it's temporary. The next book is waiting for her to leap into another world.

In her hands, the glowing key pulses, pointing her toward the next destination. She feels its pull, her fingers grazing over the spine of a thick, worn tome. The title, *The Sands of Eternity*, is etched in faded gold. She knows, without question, that this is the one.

Taking a deep breath, Emma opens the book.

The world shifts around her in a blur of golden light, and before she can blink, she feels the heat of the sun on her skin and the soft crunch of sand beneath her feet. When the light fades, she finds herself standing in the middle of an expansive desert. Towering dunes rise on all sides, and in the distance, she can see the faint outline of massive pyramids.

*Egypt.*

Emma looks down at herself, finding that her clothes have changed. Instead of her ragged coat and worn-out shoes, she's now dressed in a simple linen tunic, sandals strapped to her feet. A small satchel hangs over her shoulder, its weight reassuring, though she has no idea what it contains yet. She takes a deep breath, adjusting to the hot, dry air.

In the distance, something catches her eye. A caravan of travelers winds its way through the desert, and leading the procession is a grand chariot, its gold gleaming under the blazing sun. Behind it march soldiers, their armor reflecting the light, and in the center, shaded beneath a canopy of silken cloth, sits the pharaoh. Even from this distance, Emma can see the regal figure's crown and the intimidating staff in his hand.

The sight makes her stomach churn. This isn't just a journey through the desert, it's a challenge, a test. Her mother's voice echoes in her memory, reminding her of this story: *"To outwit the pharaoh, you must think like the gods themselves."*

A sharp movement draws Emma's attention away from the procession. A boy, no older than twelve, appears from behind a nearby dune. He's barefoot, his dark hair matted with dust, and his brown eyes glint with something between mischief and fear. His clothes are tattered, an orphan, like her.

He catches her looking and freezes, staring at her with suspicion. Emma takes a cautious step forward, holding her hands up to show she means no harm.

"Hey," Emma says, her voice calm but laced with curiosity. "Who are you?"

The boy narrows his eyes, but there's a flicker of recognition there, like he's been waiting for her. He glances toward the caravan in the distance, then back at Emma.

"Name's Kesi," he says, his voice low and quick. "I was watching you. I thought you was one of them."

Emma shakes her head. "I'm not anyone but me."

Kesi studies her for a long moment, then seems to make up his mind. "You're not like the others, either," he mutters, more to himself than to her. "Where did you come from?"

"It's a long story," Emma says, glancing over her shoulder toward the approaching caravan. "But

I'm here for the same reason you are, I think. I need to get past the pharaoh."

Kesi's eyes widen. "Outwit the pharaoh? You're crazy! No one can do that."

Emma shrugs, though she feels a tight knot of anxiety in her stomach. "Maybe. But I don't have a choice."

Kesi stares at her, then grins, his teeth flashing white against his sun-darkened skin. "Well, lucky for you, neither do I. They're after me." He gestures toward the caravan. "I'm an orphan from the city. The pharaoh's men want me for something I stole."

Kesi's life was a hard one. Abandoned at a young age, he learned quickly how to outsmart both guards and merchants to keep himself fed. His sharp wit and nimble hands made him a natural thief.

He has dark brown eyes, those eyes that are always watchful, seeming to catch every detail. He is quick, sporting a mischievous grin, often disarming those who caught him in the act. Beneath the dirty and tattered clothes, Kesi has a quiet nobility about him, a spark that speaks of someone who is destined for more than the hard life that's been dealt to him. Kesi's skin, bronzed by the sun of the desert, give him a rugged, earthy look, and his dark hair, once unruly and wild, was now neatly trimmed, though a stray curl often fell across his forehead. His lean, athletic build came from years of running through narrow streets and climbing over walls, always one step ahead of trouble.

Emma raises her eyebrows as she takes him in. "What did you steal?"

Kesi chuckles, pulling a small, intricately carved stone from his pocket. It's engraved with symbols Emma doesn't recognize, but the moment she sees it, she feels the weight of its importance.

"They call it the 'Eye of Horus,'" Kesi says, tossing it in the air and catching it again. "It's supposed to protect the pharaoh's tomb, but I figured I could use a little protection of my own."

Emma studies the stone, then looks at Kesi. "You're not planning on giving it back, are you?"

He snorts. "Not a chance."

Emma grins despite herself. She's found a kindred spirit, someone who understands what it's like to be on the run.

"So, what's the plan?" Kesi asks, his grin fading as he glances back at the approaching soldiers.

"I'm guessing you didn't just drop into the desert for a stroll."

Emma shakes her head. "I need to get into the pharaoh's tomb," she says, her voice steady but full of determination. "There's something inside that I need to unlock."

Kesi's eyes widen again. "The tomb? That's madness! The pharaoh's tomb is guarded by more than just soldiers. They say it's cursed, that anyone who enters without the pharaoh's blessing is doomed."

"I know," Emma says, her heart pounding in her chest. "But I have to try."

Kesi watches her for a long moment, then nods, his expression serious. "Well, if you're going, I guess I'm going with you. No way I'm letting those guards catch me without at least *some* mischief."

Emma feels a rush of gratitude. "Alright," she says, glancing toward the pyramids in the distance. "Let's do this."

Together, they make their way through the desert, staying low to avoid detection as they approach the pharaoh's caravan. The sun blazes overhead, and the dry hot sand shifts beneath their feet.

As they near the caravan, Emma crouches behind a dune and takes a peek over the edge of it.

The soldiers are focused on guarding the pharaoh, their eyes scanning the horizon for any sign of trouble. The chariot at the center of the procession is lavish, covered in gold and jewels, and inside, the pharaoh sits on his throne, his gaze cold and distant as he surveys the desert.

"We need a distraction," Emma whispers, glancing at Kesi. "Something to draw their attention away from the tomb."

Kesi grins, "just leave that to me."

Before Emma can stop him, Kesi sprints toward the edge of the caravan, his small form darting between the dunes. He moves like a shadow, quick and silent, until he reaches the nearest soldier. Then, with a flick of his wrist, he throws the Eye of Horus into the air.

The soldiers react instantly, their attention drawn to the gleaming stone as it sails through the air. Shouts echo through the desert, and the pharaoh's men rush forward, scrambling to retrieve the precious artifact.

"That should do it," Kesi says, appearing beside Emma with a grin. "Now's our chance!"

They sprint toward the tomb, the soldiers too distracted by the Eye of Horus to notice them slipping past. The entrance to the tomb is grand, carved into the base of the largest pyramid, its stone doors engraved with ancient symbols and hieroglyphics.

Emma's heart races as they reach the entrance. The key in her hand glows brighter, its light pulsing in time with her heartbeat.

She steps forward, holding the key out in front of her. The stone doors tremble, and with a loud creak, they begin to open, revealing a dark, yawning corridor that leads deep into the pyramid.

Kesi glances at Emma, his grin fading. "You sure about this?"

Emma nods, though her stomach twists with nerves. "We have to go inside. The answers are in there."

Together, they step into the tomb, the air cool and heavy around them. The corridor stretches out before them, lined with towering statues and flickering torches. Every step they take echoes through the stone walls, the weight of the pharaoh's curse pressing down on them.

As they venture deeper into the tomb, Emma feels the pull of the memories growing stronger. They're close—so close to unlocking the next piece of the puzzle. But she knows there will be challenges ahead, traps laid by the pharaoh to protect his secrets.

Suddenly, the ground beneath them trembles, and the stone walls shift, closing in on them. Emma's heart races as she realizes they've triggered something—something ancient and dangerous.

"Run!" Kesi shouts, grabbing her arm and pulling her forward as the walls begin to close in.

They sprint through the corridor, the ground shaking beneath them, the air thick with dust and the echo of the pharaoh's curse. Emma's pulse pounds in her ears, but she knows they can't stop now.

The walls tremble, stone grinding against stone as Emma and Kesi sprint through the dark corridor, their footsteps echoing in the tomb's suffocating silence. Every heartbeat feels like a countdown, the walls inching closer with every second.

"Faster!" Kesi shouts, his voice edged with panic.

Emma's breath comes in ragged gasps, the thick air of the tomb filling her lungs like lead. Her feet slap against the uneven stone floor, and the key pulses in her hand, its light growing brighter as they race deeper into the labyrinth of the pharaoh's final resting place.

Ahead, the corridor splits in two directions, one passage leading deeper into darkness, the other toward a faint flicker of torchlight. Emma doesn't hesitate. She tugs Kesi toward the light, her instincts screaming that the answer lies in the direction where the air feels less oppressive.

They barrel through the passage, the walls narrowing around them, but the oppressive grinding of stone fades behind them. For now, they're safe. But Emma knows it's temporary. This tomb is riddled with traps, ancient magic woven into every corner to keep intruders away from the secrets it guards.

As they emerge into a small chamber, Emma stops, her chest heaving. Kesi doubles over, his hands on his knees as he struggles to catch his breath.

The chamber is lit by flickering torches mounted on the walls, casting long shadows that dance across the stone floor. In the center of the room stands a statue of Anubis, the jackal-headed god of death, towering over them with an imposing gaze. Its eyes follow their every move, as though watching, waiting.

"This place..." Kesi pants, glancing around the chamber with wide eyes. "It's alive."

Emma doesn't argue. The entire tomb feels like it's aware of them, reacting to their presence. The air itself hums with ancient energy, and the weight of centuries presses down on her chest.

"It's not just a tomb," Emma whispers, stepping closer to the statue. "It's a trap."

Kesi straightens, wiping the sweat from his brow. "What now? We just keep running until the place decides to crush us?"

Emma shakes her head, her eyes scanning the chamber. "No. There's a puzzle here. There always is." She lifts the glowing key in her hand, watching as its light reflects off the statue's polished surface. "The pharaoh wouldn't just bury his secrets. He would've made sure only someone worthy could find them."

Kesi raises an eyebrow. "And how do we prove we're worthy? I'm not exactly a fan of ancient curses."

Emma moves toward the statue of Anubis, her heart pounding as she approaches the base of the pedestal. The key in her hand grows warmer, its glow intensifying. There's something here, something important.

Then she sees a series of small carvings etched into the base of the statue. Hieroglyphics, some worn by time, but still legible. Emma's fingers trace the symbols, her mind working to translate the ancient language.

"It's a riddle," she says, her voice barely above a whisper. "To pass, we must answer it."

Kesi groans. "Great. What's it says?"

Emma's brow furrows as she reads the hieroglyphs aloud: *"The one who seeks eternity must outwit death. But to find what is lost, you must give what you hold most dear. What will you sacrifice to enter the afterlife?"*

Kesi falls silent, his eyes narrowing as he stares at the riddle. "That doesn't sound good."

Emma's heart sinks. She knows what the riddle is asking. The pharaoh's tomb isn't about solving puzzles; it's about sacrifice. To reach the treasure hidden within, she has to give up something precious. But what could that be? What do they have to offer that's valuable enough to satisfy a king who took his wealth with him into the afterlife?

Kesi shifts uneasily beside her, his hands slipping into his pockets. "Sacrifice? What do they expect us to give? I don't have anything."

Emma looks down at the glowing key in her hand, its soft light pulsing in time with her heartbeat. The key is part of the answer, she knows that.

But she's not sure if it's enough. The pharaoh's riddle is asking for something more personal.

And then it hits her.

"The memories," Emma whispers, her eyes widening. "That's what I have to give."

Kesi looks at her, confused. "What do you mean?"

"The memories I've unlocked," Emma explains, her voice trembling slightly. "The ones I've been carrying with me. The pharaoh's asking me to give up the very thing I came here to find."

The weight of her realization settles over her like a heavy cloak. The memories of her mother, of the stories she's clung to, are the most precious things she has. They've guided her through this journey, given her the strength to keep going. And now, she's being asked to give them up.

She hesitates, her heart aching at the thought of losing them. The memories are all she has left of her mother; of the life she once knew. But she understands now, this is the ultimate test. To unlock the tomb's secrets, she has to be willing to let go of the past, to sacrifice what she holds most dear.

With trembling hands, Emma raises the glowing key toward the statue of Anubis. The light flares, bright and blinding, and for a moment, the air hums with ancient power.

"I'll give the memories," she says, her voice barely above a whisper. "I'll sacrifice them."

The statue's eyes seem to gleam in response, and a deep rumble shakes the chamber as the stone beneath their feet shifts. The hieroglyphs glow with an eerie light, and the ground beneath them opens, revealing a hidden passageway that descends into the darkness below.

Kesi stares at the opening, his eyes wide with disbelief. "You did it."

Emma nods, though her heart feels heavy. She can feel the weight of her sacrifice, the loss of the memories she's carried with her. But she knows it's the only way forward.

"Come on," she says, her voice soft but determined. "We have to keep going."

Together, they descend into the darkness of the passageway, the air growing cooler and more oppressive the deeper they go. The glow of the key has dimmed, but its warmth still guides Emma forward.

As they reach the bottom of the passage, they find themselves in another chamber, this one far larger than the first. Massive stone sarcophagi line the walls, and in the center of the room sits a golden chest, its surface engraved with intricate symbols.

Kesi whistles softly, his eyes wide as he takes in the sight. "This is it, isn't it? The pharaoh's treasure."

Emma steps forward, her heart racing. The chest gleams in the faint light, its surface untouched by time. She knows that inside lies the final piece of the puzzle, the key to unlocking the memories that will help her leave the library.

But as she reaches for the chest, the ground trembles beneath their feet.

A low, growling voice echoes through the chamber, sending a chill down Emma's spine. "You have come far, but not far enough."

Emma freezes, her hand hovering over the chest. The air grows thick with tension, and from the shadows of the chamber, a figure emerges all tall and cloaked in darkness, with glowing eyes that burn like fire.

"The pharaoh's guardian," Kesi whispers, his voice trembling. "We're not alone."

The guardian steps closer, its presence oppressive, and Emma knows they're about to face their greatest challenge yet. She steals herself, her pulse quickening as she grips the key tightly in her hand.

# Chapter 10: The Chimes of Time

A sudden, sharp chime pierces the air, clear and insistent. Emma flinches, her hand recoiling from the chest as the sound reverberates through the chamber. It's a clock, tolling somewhere deep in the tomb, though no clock belongs in this ancient place. Each strike feels like a pulse in her chest, growing louder, more urgent, reminding her that time is slipping away.

*Kesi can't hear it*; she realizes as she glances over at him. He's focused on the guardian, frozen in fear, his wide eyes locked on the towering figure. The chime sounds again, louder this time, like an invisible clock marking the moments she has left. It echoes off the stone walls, but Kesi doesn't react. The boy doesn't even flinch.

"Emma?" Kesi whispers, his voice trembling. "What do we do? It's... coming closer."

But Emma isn't listening to him. Her mind is fixed on the clock, on the relentless ticking of time that only she can hear. The library is reminding her—*hurry or be trapped*. It's the same warning, the same rule that has followed her from story to story:

*Return before dawn. Return before the clock runs out..*

The air around them grows colder, and the figure steps forward again, its glowing eyes narrowing as it blocks their path. The guardian of the tomb, an ancient force that doesn't belong in any story she's ever heard. A low, guttural growl rumbles from its chest, and Emma knows they're out of time.

"We need to go," Emma says, her voice tight as she grabs Kesi's arm and pulls him back, away from the chest. "**Now**."

"What?" Kesi yanks his arm free, confusion and panic flashing across his face. "We haven't gotten the treasure yet! What are you talking about?"

Another chime sounds, cutting through her thoughts. The pressure in her chest tightens. She shakes her head, knowing that no treasure is worth being trapped in this tomb forever. "It's not about the treasure. There's no time."

The guardian moves closer, its massive form casting a long shadow over them. Emma's heart pounds as she grips Kesi's arm again, this time more urgently. She can feel the pull of the library, dragging her back, calling her away from this world before it's too late. But Kesi doesn't feel he's stuck in this story, and if she leaves him here, he'll be caught, left to face the pharaoh's wrath. Or worse, the tomb's curse.

"Kesi," she says, her voice cracking, "if you stay here, you'll be killed. The pharaoh won't spare you."

His eyes widen with fear, and for a moment, he's just a scared boy again, an orphan like her, alone and desperate. "I... I don't have anywhere else to go, Emma. Egypt is my home, but they're hunting me. If I leave this tomb, they'll find me."

The chime rings again, louder this time, making Emma's whole-body tremble. She closes her eyes, trying to block out the relentless ticking. There's no time to explain everything, no time to tell Kesi about the library or the magic that binds them to these stories. She can't leave him here, not like this. But she can't take him with her either, he doesn't belong in her world.

*Or could he?* A thought flickers in her mind, one that sends a chill through her. She has the power to leave this story, to move through the library's endless shelves and enter different worlds. Kesi could come with her, but it wouldn't be to her life, not the one outside the library. She could put him in another book, a safer one, a world where he wouldn't be hunted or trapped in an endless curse.

"Kesi, I can help you," she says, her voice soft but firm. "I can take you somewhere better. Somewhere safe."

He stares at her, confused. "What do you mean? How?"

Emma swallows, her throat dry. "You wouldn't understand, but I can take you to another place. A different story. Somewhere where the pharaoh's men can't find you."

Kesi's eyes widen with hope, but there's doubt too. "You can just... take me somewhere else? Like magic?"

She nods, though her stomach churns with uncertainty. She's not even sure if this will work, she's never tried to bring someone with her from one world to another. But she knows she can't leave him here. "Yes. But you'll have to trust me."

The guardian's growl deepens, its massive form stepping closer still. The clock chimes once more, the sound pressing into her skull. They have to go now.

"I trust you," Kesi says quickly, desperation clear in his voice. "Take me with you, Emma. I don't care where, just don't leave me here."

Emma nods, gripping his hand tightly. "Hold on."

With a deep breath, she closes her eyes and reaches for the pull of the library, the invisible thread that connects her to the stories, to the next leap. The key in her hand flares with light, and she feels the world shift around her, the stone floor vanishing beneath her feet as they fall through the veil of magic, away from the tomb, away from the pharaoh's curse.

For a moment, everything is dark, the air heavy with silence. Grasping a book nearby on the same shelf. The book entitled; *Egypt and the Village of Peace,* she quickly opens the book with Kesi, still holding hands.

---

When Emma opens her eyes, she finds herself standing in a new world, the soft glow of lamplight casting warm shadows over cobblestone streets. The smell of fresh bread and the sound of distant laughter fill the air, and for the first time since entering the library, Emma feels a sense of calm wash over her. The world around her is peaceful and safe.

Kesi stands beside her, his eyes wide with awe as he takes in the scene. "Where... where are we?"

Emma glances around, her heart settling as she realizes where the new book has taken them.

It's a quaint, sleepy town, with stone cottages lining the streets and children running through the square. A small, peaceful village, far from the chaos of Egypt, far from the dangers of the pharaoh's men.

"You'll be safe here," Emma says, her voice soft. "No one will come after you."

Kesi looks at her, disbelief and gratitude shining in his eyes. "You did it. You really brought me somewhere else."

Emma smiles, though the weight of what she's about to do presses heavily on her heart. "You can stay here, Kesi. You'll be okay now."

But as she says the words, a new thought creeps into her mind; *what if she stayed too?* She could stay in one of these stories, in a place like this, where there's laughter and light.

Kesi watches her, the hope in his eyes dimming as he notices her hesitation. "Aren't you... aren't you staying too?"

Emma bites her lip, uncertainty tugging at her. For a moment, the idea of staying tempts her. She could rewrite her fate, live in a world where she mattered, where she wasn't abandoned or forgotten.

But deep down, she knows it's not right. These worlds aren't hers. They're stories, and as much as she wants to escape, she has her own story to finish.

"I can't stay," Emma says softly, her voice thick with emotion. "I have to go back."

Kesi frowns, confusion clouding his expression. "Why? Why would you go back to a place where no one cares about you? You could stay here, Emma. You could have a life here."

Emma feels tears sting her eyes, but she shakes her head. "Because... it's my life. It's not perfect, but it's mine. And I need to finish what I started. I hope I can come to visit you again once this is all over. But I am sorry you lost your amulet because of me."

Kesi looks at her for a long moment, then nods slowly, understanding settling in his eyes. "I'll never forget what you did for me, Emma. But not to worry," he takes the amulet out of his pocket. "I wasn't about to give this up that easily. The other object I threw was colored glass." He laughed.

She smiles and laughs too, though her heart aches. " You are very clever. Well, take care of yourself, okay?"

He nods, stepping back as Emma turns to face the invisible pull of the library once more. The chime of the clock echoes faintly in the distance,

but this time, it feels less urgent, more like a reminder than a threat.

With one last glance at the peaceful village,
Emma takes a deep breath and closes her eyes, letting the library's magic sweep her away.

As the familiar pull of the library sweeps over
her, Emma feels herself slipping away from the
peaceful village and back into the swirling, endless
depths of the library. The warmth of the lamplight,
the sounds of children laughing all fade, leaving only the cold, quiet emptiness of the library's towering
shelves.

The library's usual stillness is gone, replaced
by an unsettling tension that crackles in the air. The
shelves around her loom higher than ever before,
their spines darker, the books more ancient and
worn. Shadows seem to move on their own, crawl-
ing along the floor and walls as if alive.

Emma frowns, her heart quickening. The air
feels thick, like the weight of a storm about to
break. And then, she hears a faint, almost imper-
ceptible sound. The ticking of a clock, distant but
growing louder with every second.

She freezes, her breath catching in her
throat. The chimes had always been a warning, a
reminder that time was running out, but this sound
is different. It's not just a warning, it's a countdown.

And for the first time, Emma feels true fear grip her heart.

The ticking grows louder, echoing off the shelves and filling the space around her. Panic flares in her chest, and she spins around, searching for the source. But there's no clock, no visible sign of what's making the noise. Just the endless rows of books, their spines pressing in on her like the walls of a cage.

"Time is slipping away," a voice whispers, low and cold.

Emma stiffens, her blood running cold. The voice isn't hers, and it doesn't belong to the library. It's something else watching her, hidden in the shadows of this strange place.

"Who's there?" Emma calls out, her voice shaky as she grips the glowing key in her hand. Its light flickers weakly, as though struggling to stay alive in the oppressive darkness. "Show yourself!"

Silence. Then, the voice again, closer now.

"You think you've been moving through stories... unlocking memories. But it's not your journey you've been following, Emma. It's mine."

A figure steps out from between the shelves, cloaked in shadow. Emma takes a step back, her pulse quickening as she watches the figure approach. She can't see its face, only the dark outline of a tall, lean form, and the cold air that swirls around it.

"I've been watching you," the figure says, its voice soft and mocking. "Every leap you've taken, every puzzle you've solved. You've been playing my game."

Emma's heart pounds in her chest. "Who are you?" She demands, the fear creeping into her voice. "What do you want?"

The figure laughs, a sound that sends a shiver down her spine. "You still don't understand, do you? This library... it's not just a place of stories. It's a prison. And you've been running through it, trying to escape, but you NEVER will. Not without me."

Emma feels the world tilt beneath her. A prison? She shakes her head, her mind racing. "No, I've been unlocking the past, finding my way out. I'm ..following a trail, I left for you," the figure interrupts, stepping closer. "The memories you've been chasing, the puzzles you've been solving, they're not yours. They're mine."

She looks down at the key in her hand, its weak glow reflecting the doubt now swirling in her mind. Everything she's done, every challenge she's faced, it was all part of a larger plan. But not her plan.

The figure's shadowy form shifts, and for the first time, Emma can make out its face. Her breath catches in her throat. It's... familiar. The same sharp features, the same eyes. It's like looking into a twisted mirror.

The reflection figure is her.

Or, rather, a version of her. Older. Darker. Twisted by something she can't fully understand.

"I was like you once," the figure says, its cold eyes gleaming. "An orphan, lost in the stories, chasing after a way out. But I learned the truth. This library isn't a refuge. It's a trap, and the only way to escape it is to control it."

Emma stumbles back, her heart racing. "No... you're lying. I've been finding my memories, my past. I've been.."

"Unlocking the doors I wanted you to unlock," the figure snaps, its voice sharp. "You've been my pawn, Emma. Every world you entered, every book you leaped into, was because I allowed it. I need you to free me."

Emma's mind reels. None of this makes sense. How could she have been manipulated, led through stories that weren't hers? She thinks back to Kesi, to the haunted mansion, to the dragon, all of it felt real, tied to her past.

But now, the lines between truth and illusion blur.

"I don't believe you," Emma says, her voice trembling but firm. "I've felt the memories. They're mine."

The figure smiles, a cruel, mocking smile that sends a chill through Emma's bones. "Are they? Or are they what I wanted you to believe? You were scared when I chased you in the forest."

The ticking of the clock grows louder, pounding in Emma's ears. The shadows around them seem to deepen, closing in on her, suffocating her. The pressure builds in her chest, and for the first time since entering the library, she feels completely lost.

The figure steps closer, its eyes gleaming with dark intent. "Time is running out, Emma. You can either help me escape, or you'll be trapped here forever, just like I am."

Emma shakes her head, her thoughts spiraling. The library, the place she thought was guiding her, helping her unlock her past, was something far more sinister. And now, this twisted version of herself, this shadow, is asking her to make a choice.

Her mind races, but the clock's chimes grow louder, drowning out her thoughts. Time is slipping away, and she's no closer to finding the truth.

*But she* thinks *the truth doesn't matter anymore. What matters is what I choose.*

Emma steadies herself, tightening her grip on the key. She takes a deep breath, staring at the twisted figure that wears her face.

"I don't care what you've planned for me," Emma says, her voice stronger now. "I'm not your pawn, and I won't let you control me."

The figure's smile falters, just for a moment, before it twists into a sneer. "You think you can defy me? You think you can walk away from this?"

"I don't have to walk away," Emma says, her heart pounding. "I just have to choose what's real for me. And this...you...you're not real."

The figure steps forward, its face contorting with fury, but Emma doesn't flinch. She raises the key, feeling its warmth spread through her hand, and takes a deep breath. The clock chimes again, but this time, it sounds different, less threatening, more like a countdown to something new.

"I choose to keep going," Emma says, her voice steady. "To find my way out of this place. Without you."

The figure's eyes burn with anger and hears her screams, but Emma doesn't give it a chance to continue to taunt her. She closes her eyes rubbing the key, she then can feel the pull of the library one more time. The world around her spins, and the figure's furious scream fades into the distance.

As the chimes of the clock fade, Emma feels the weight lift from her chest. She's still in the library, but this time, the shadows around her don't seem dark. The endless shelves stretch out before her, but they no longer feel like a prison.

---

# Chapter 11: Through the Pages

The jungle in this story she jumped into had pressed hard on Emma from all sides, the air thick with humidity, the scent of damp earth and rotting foliage filling her lungs with every shallow breath. Tall trees loomed above her, their thick branches twisted and gnarled, reaching out like skeletal hands to blot out the sky. The dense canopy allowed only slivers of light to filter through, casting the jungle floor an array of shifting patterns in the darkness. Vines hung like serpents from the trees, their tendrils winding around Emma's arms and legs as she struggled, helplessly ensnared by the trap that had been set for her. Her decision to open the eye book was a horrible mistake. It served no purpose but to hurt her.

The trap had been invisible, until it wasn't.

One wrong step, one misplaced foot, and the ground beneath her had given way, sending her crashing into the pit below. The vines had snapped to life, binding her wrists and ankles, tightening their grip with every breath she took. She could barely move, the thick ropes of greenery cutting into her skin as she twisted and pulled, her heart pounding in her chest.

Emma's mind raced, her thoughts muddled by panic and exhaustion. She'd faced countless dangers before, but this felt different. This jungle wasn't like the other worlds she had visited. There was something alive in the air, something watching, waiting. And now, trapped and alone, the weight of her isolation pressed down on her. It was coming for her.

"Kesi..." she whispered under her breath; her voice barely audible in the dense silence. He wasn't here. He was in another book, another story, far away, unreachable.

She had ventured into this jungle alone, confident she could manage the challenge, but now, faced with the crushing reality of the trap, she realized just how much she needed him.

A sharp pain shot through her wrist as she tried to free herself again, her fingers clawing at the vines. Her breath came in shallow gasps, her chest tightening with the growing sense of helplessness.

The jungle seemed to close in on her, the trees swaying ominously in the windless air. Just as she pulled against the tightening vines, a faint rustling sound reached her ears. Emma turned her head slowly, her heart hammering in her chest. Emerging from the dense foliage was a massive, hairy spider, its legs as long as her arm, creeping toward her with terrifying silence. Its many eyes glistened in the darkness, each one reflecting her growing terror as its fangs twitched hungrily. Emma's pulse quickened as the spider's heavy legs crunched over leaves, drawing closer with every slow, deliberate step. She called out again, this time much louder, her voice tinged with desperation.

And somewhere, deep in the recesses of the library, he heard her.

---

Kesi stood in the middle of a vast desert, the wind whipping sand around his feet as he squinted against the glaring sun. He had been tracking something—a relic of a forgotten age that was supposed to hold the key to unlocking another layer of the library's secrets. But now, everything felt wrong. The desert's heat pressed down on him like a weight, but it wasn't the desert about which he was concerned.

*It was Emma!*

A strange pull tightened in his chest, an invisible thread that tugged at his very core. It was faint at first, barely noticeable, but now it had grown stronger, more insistent, like a voice calling out to him from the edges of his mind. Emma was in danger. He could feel it. The bond they shared, forged over countless adventures, was deeper than just love—it was a connection that spanned worlds.

Her voice echoed faintly in his ears, blowing the wind, though she was nowhere to be seen.

He spun around, scanning the endless horizon of dunes, his heart racing. She was in trouble, trapped somewhere, and every instinct he had screamed for him to reach her. But how? They were in different books, different stories entirely. The library had taken them on separate paths this time, their journeys diverging for reasons even he didn't fully understand.

But he didn't care. He wouldn't let her face this alone.

"Kesi!" her voice came again, louder this time, and Kesi's heart leapt into his throat.

He closed his eyes, steadying himself, focusing on the pull of the library, the invisible thread that connected him to Emma. The library itself was alive, a force that moved and shifted with its own will, but Kesi had learned how to navigate its strange magic. He had learned how to listen to it, how to feel its pulse. And now, it was calling him, guiding him toward Emma.

Without hesitation, Kesi turned and ran, his feet kicking up clouds of sand as he sprinted across the desert. He could feel the library shifting around him, its pages folding and unfolding, bending the rules of space and time. He wasn't running toward any specific place. He was running through the stories themselves, pushing through the fabric of the books, leaping from one world to another in his race to find her.

The warm desert air suddenly turned cool and humid, and Kesi felt the ground beneath him change from sand to a damp dense forest. He emerges, the air thick with the scent of moss and wet leaves. Emma's voice was closer now, sharp with fear, and Kesi's heart raced.

"Emma!" he yelled out, pushing through a wall of vines.

He broke into a small clearing and saw her, she was bound by thick, writhing vines, her wrists were red from struggling. Dirt and sweat clung to her face and body. But Kesi's eyes widened as he saw what loomed over her, a massive, hairy spider, its eyes gleaming with a predatory glint and venom dripping from its fangs. It was easily the size of a horse, its long legs silently inching closer to Emma.

Without thinking, Kesi reached for the dagger at his side. He didn't know if a simple blade would be enough to stop the creature, but he wasn't about to let that spider get any closer to her.

"Hey!" Kesi shouted, waving the dagger, and began running toward the spider.

The creature turned, its many eyes locking onto him. Kesi could see the true size of the creature, and for a moment, he felt a flicker of doubt. But Emma's frightened eyes gave him the courage he needed.

With a roar, Kesi lunged forward, slashing at one of the spider's front legs. The creature hissed, the sound echoing through the jungle, and reared back, its injured leg twitching. Kesi stumbled on a root in the ground but managed to regain his footing; his heart pounding in his ears.

"Kesi, look out!" Emma screamed.

The spider lunged at him, its fangs snapping dangerously close. Kesi ducked and rolled to the side, coming up in a crouch with his dagger held ready. The creature's legs shifted, preparing to strike again, and Kesi could see it assessing him, calculating its next move.

"Kesi, stab it in the eyes!" Emma called; her voice urgent.

Kesi charged at the spider, aiming for its closest eye. The creature reared back, but not quickly enough—Kesi's blade connected, piercing the spider's eye with a sickening crunch. The creature shrieked, a high-pitched, almost human-like wail, and stumbled back, its legs flailing.

Taking advantage of the creatures disorientation, Kesi slashed at another leg, and the spider's massive body sagged, its movements turning sluggish. He kept slashing, dodging its frantic strikes, and each cut weakened the creature further.

Finally, with a desperate lunge, Kesi drove his dagger into the spider's head. The creature twitched once, then collapsed, its legs curling inward as it let out a final hiss. Kesi wiped himself that was covered with the spiders webs. His breathing labored, the adrenaline making his hands shake.

"Are you okay?" he asked, rushing to Emma's side.

She nodded, her face pale from shock. "The vines, cut the vines," she urged.

Kesi quickly sliced through the vines that held her, and Emma pulled her wrists free, rubbing them gingerly. "Thanks," she breathed, offering him a shaky smile. "That was... *intense*."

Kesi let out a relieved laugh, wiping the dirt and sweat from his brow. "I'd say so."

"Kesi," Emma said, her voice quiet but resolute. "I think I am running out of time."

Kesi nodded, gripping his dagger tightly. "Then let's keep moving."

Emma leaned into him; her breath shaky but relieved. "How... how did you find me?"

Kesi met her gaze, his eyes softening as he looked at her. "I heard you, Emma. The library and my amulet, it helped me, it led me here."

Emma's chest tightened with emotion. Even though they had been separated by worlds, he had come for her, crossing through countless stories without hesitation, risking everything to save her.

Kesi pulled her into his arms, holding her tightly against his chest, the warmth of his embrace filling her with a sense of safety she hadn't felt in years. "You're safe now," he whispered into her hair. "I'll always find you. No matter what. Take my hand, and I will return you to the library."

For a moment, Emma let herself relax, breathing in the familiar scent of old parchment and the faint hint of desert winds that always seemed to cling to Kesi.

"Are you sure we can find our way back?" Emma asked, her voice barely above a whisper, still feeling the echoes of the spider's hiss in her ears.

Kesi smiled down at her, holding the stolen amulet. A mischievous spark in his eyes. "If I could steal the Eye of Horus and kill a massive spider, then taking you back is a piece of cake," he said, squeezing her hand reassuringly.

The Eye of Horus was a small and it glistened in Kesi's hand, an intricately carved amulet, made of polished lapis lazuli, its deep blue surface etched with delicate lines forming the eye's unmistakable shape. The amulet's center held a small, circular gemstone that glimmered faintly, as if a hidden light pulsed within. Legend spoke of its ability to bend the threads of reality and connect the wearer to different realms, offering protection and a passage between worlds.

By holding the Eye of Horus and closing their eyes, Kesi and Emma could harness its ancient magic to return to the library. It allowed them to focus on the invisible pull of the library's heart, guiding them back through stories and space as effortlessly as turning a page. All they needed was to touch the amulet and concentrate, and the Eye would shift the world around them, carrying them safely home.

"Now, let's get out of here before that spider's family shows up." Kesi laughed and held Emma's hand; the world they were in begins to drift away.

---

# Chapter 12: Her Story

The library stretches out before Emma, an infinite maze of possibilities. She passes familiar titles, books that once called to her with their mysteries and puzzles, but now they seem like echoes of someone else's story.

As she turns a corner, something catches her eye large, open book resting on a podium at the far end of a dimly lit alcove. Its pages are spread wide, and the air around it seems to hum with quiet anticipation. Emma feels the pull again, but this time it's different. It's not dragging her into a world of someone else's making. It's calling her to something more personal. Something she needs to see.

Her steps quicken as she approaches the podium. The book is old, its leather cover cracked and worn from countless hands that must have touched it over the years. But it's the words on the pages that stop Emma from her tracks.

It's her story.

Her breath catches in her throat as her eyes skim the pages. Every moment she's experienced in the library is written there, line by line. The dragon's challenge, the haunted mansion, outwitting the pharaoh, all of it is written with perfect clarity, as though the library itself has been recording her every move. Emma's hands tremble as she flips the pages, watching her own journey unfold before her eyes. She reads that Kesi is safe in another story, that makes her happy.

And then, the writing stops.

The last page is blank, waiting.

Emma stares at the empty space, her heart racing. The library has been telling her story up until now. The weight of it presses down on her, but there's also a thrill in it. For the first time, she's not just a part of the library's endless web of stories. She's the author. She holds the pen.

Slowly, she reaches out and touches the quill resting beside the book, its feathers soft and delicate. Her fingers curl around it, and as she lifts it from the inkwell, she feels a surge of energy course through her. The key in her pocket pulses faintly, as if urging her forward, but this time, the choice is hers.

Emma's eyes drift to the blank page, and she takes a deep breath.

*What do I want?*

The answer comes slowly at first, but then it floods her mind, filling her with clarity. She's spent so long chasing memories, trying to escape the life of an orphan, trying to unlock the secrets of the past. But now she understands that her journey isn't about leaving behind who she was, it's about embracing who she can become.

She dips the quill into the ink and begins to write.

"I am not just an orphan. I am more than the girl who lost her family, more than the child who waited for someone to find her. I am the one who chooses my own path. And I choose to write a new story, one where every child, every orphan, has a place to belong."

The words flow easily, the ink gliding across the page as Emma writes with purpose. She writes about finding homes for all the children like her, children who have been lost in the shuffle, who feel invisible in a world that seems to have forgotten them. She writes about a place where no one is left behind, where every orphan can find safety, love, and a family.

"I will find homes for all the orphans, including me," she writes, her heart pounding. "I will build a world where we are no longer lost or forgotten. Where we are seen, heard, and loved."

The quill scratches across the paper, filling the page with her vision, her hope. She writes about the others she's met along the way, especially Kesi. She writes about other worlds, other stories, where she will place each child in her orphanage and be placed in a safe and loving home, in worlds where they can thrive.

The more she writes, the more her vision solidifies and becomes crystal clear. The library, she realizes, has the power to create endless possibilities. It has the power to shape lives, to offer second chances. And Emma will use that power to rewrite the destinies of every orphan, including her own.

But there's something else. A deeper, more personal desire.

Emma pauses, the quill hovering over the page. She's written so much about the other children, about giving them homes and families. But what about her? Where does her story end?

The answer comes softly, like a whisper in her mind. Emma writes slowly, deliberately.

"I choose to have a family of my own. I choose to find a home where I belong. I won't be alone anymore."

Tears are forming in her eyes as she writes.

The moment she finishes writing, the book glows softly, the ink glows as the library itself seems to acknowledge her decision. The key in her pocket warms, as though it's been waiting for this moment all along.

Emma steps back, her heart full. She's no longer just a girl trapped in someone else's story or in this library. She's the writer of her own fate.

The library shifts around her, the shadows pulling back as if the very walls are breathing with relief. Emma smiles, feels a weight lifted.

She places the quill back on the podium, watching as the words she's written shimmer and dry on the page. The book remains open, but the future is hers to fill out. Her destiny isn't bound to any one story; she is the master of her own tale.

As she turns to leave the alcove, she hears the soft, comforting hum of the library. Like a soft melody.

The sound of the ticking of the clock has stopped. The library now glows with soft warm lights. The door opens. She can come and go whenever she wishes.

Time is no longer her enemy; it never really was.

# Chapter 13: The Last Adventure

A soft white glow of ancient lamps now cast warm shadows over all of the books, and the faint hum of the library's magic lingers in the air like an old friend.

Emma smiles as she steps through the door of the library, her fingers brushing the worn spines of the countless books that line the shelves. It's been many years since she had first stumbled into this place, frightened and unsure. The library is like an old friend, and she visits often. Even as she grows older and her life shifts in the outside world this is her sanctuary.

She's different now from the little orphan girl who used to wander these halls, searching for memories and a way out. She's all grown up, and found her place in the world, plus a home filled with love and laughter. The old library will always call to her, and she can't resist coming back for more adventures, especially today, before the gift arrives.

Today, Emma chooses a special book, an old kingdom—medieval, grand, and full of mysteries. Complete with giant flying geese to ride on.

The thought makes her laugh softly as she recalls her last visit so long ago. A kingdom perched on the edge of a cliff, with wild geese soaring high above the towering castles. It had been one of her most exciting adventures, and even now, the idea of riding one of those massive geese again fills her with a sense of wonder she never quite outgrew.

The title glimmers in gold: *The Lost Kingdom of Amaranth.*

A wide smile spreads across her face as she pulls the book from the shelf. The weight of it in her hands feels comforting, like holding a piece of magic. She runs her fingers over the gilded pages, already hearing the flap of wings and feeling the rush of wind against her skin. This is the adventure she needs today.

Emma finds her favorite chair, an old dusty plush burgundy armchair all tucked away in a quiet corner of the library, and she settles in, the book resting on her lap. She closes her eyes, with the amulet hung delicately around her neck, takes a deep breath, and lets the world around her fall away as she opens the book.

She opens her eyes again, and she's soaring.

The sky around Emma is a breathtaking canvas of color, the endless blue stretches into infinity. But it's the clouds that catch her attention first, massive, pillowy formations that swirl like spun sugar, glowing with hues of gold and pink as the setting sun casts its light upon them. It's as if the sky itself has been painted with a brush dipped in stardust.

Emma holds tightly to the soft, feathered neck of the giant goose beneath her. Its wings are immense, easily ten feet across, each feathers highlights are shimmering like polished gold in the sunlight. The bird's body is sleek, its pure white feathers so bright they glow, a faint iridescence trailing off its wings as it glides through the air. Its eyes are large, crystal blue and intelligent. A deep, calming blue that mirrors the sky above, and its long, graceful neck curves elegantly as it flies. There's a softness to the creature's body, a warmth in its feathers, making Emma feel safe.

The air rushes past her face, cool and sweet, carrying with it the scent of jasmine, a scent that shouldn't belong in the open sky, but here, in this magical place, they fit perfectly. Beneath her, the kingdom of Amaranth sprawls in a shimmering expanse.

The entire kingdom is built among the towering cliffs that just out from the clouds it stands, like islands floating in the sky. Massive waterfalls cascade from the cliffs, their water sparkling with shades of emerald and sapphire as they tumble down into the mist below, disappearing into a sea of white fog. The waterfalls don't crash, they flow like rivers in the air, suspended between the sky and land. It's as though gravity works differently here, allowing the kingdom to hover, suspended in the heavens.

At the highest point of the kingdom stands the royal castle, a masterpiece of ethereal architecture. Its spires are impossibly tall, reaching so high they touch the edges of the stars. Each tower is made of gleaming marble that shifts color with the light, from pearly white in the day to soft lavender and deep indigo as the sun sets. Crystalline bridges connect the towers, arching gracefully between them, and the windows of the castle reflect the sky, giving the entire structure an almost translucent appearance, as if the castle itself could disappear into the clouds at any moment.

The kingdom's streets wind in and out of the cliffs, carved directly into the rock faces, but every building is topped with spiraling roofs made of a brilliant turquoise stone, speckled with gold. The homes and shops shimmer like gems, nestled against the cliffs and lining the waterfalls, connected by delicate rope bridges that sway gently in the breeze. Flocks of geese, smaller than the one Emma rides, but just as majestic, soar between the cliffs, their wings trailing arcs of soft, glowing light.

Below, the streets are busy with life. Market stalls overflow with vibrant fruits and exotic flowers, their colors so bright they almost seem to glow, while vendors call out to customers in a language Emma doesn't understand.

Emma's goose lets out a soft honk, and she feels the rush of wind beneath its wings as it angles upward, flying higher and faster toward the floating castle. The movement is effortless, like the bird is in perfect harmony with the sky itself. Emma leans into the wind, laughing as she feels the exhilaration of flight.

The sun begins to set, painting the sky in deep shades of crimson and violet. The clouds glow with soft oranges and pinks, their edges lit by the fading light, and the kingdom below is bathed in a golden glow that makes everything seem more alive, more magical. The waterfalls catch the light, turning into streams of liquid fire as they flow down the cliffs.

The trees glow with a soft, internal light emerald, green, royal blue, fiery orange pulsing gently like the beating of a heart. Their leaves shimmer in the air, and as the wind moves through them, they release a soft tinkling sound, like the gentle chime of bells in the distance.

Emma feels the goose beneath her shift, its body angling toward one of the castle's grand balconies. As they approach, the enormous stone platform seems to rise to meet them, its surface glowing faintly with runes carved into the floor. A light breeze tugs at the curtains that billow from the balcony's arched windows, and standing there, waiting for her, is the king.

Tall and imposing, the King of Amaranth wears a crown made of pure silver, set with jewels that sparkle with their own internal light. His robes are a deep royal blue, edged with gold, and his eyes, like the sky above, are full of wisdom and kindness. He gestures for Emma to dismount, and she does, her feet touching the cool, smooth stone of the balcony as her heart pounds with excitement.

"Welcome back, Emma," the King says, his voice rich and warm. "We've been waiting for you."

"Always happy to be here." Emma says as she bows.

For hours, Emma loses herself in the adventure, exploring hidden passageways, flying with the geese, solving riddles to unlock the castle's long-forgotten secrets. It's been a wonderful day.

Emma smiles, her breath catching as she looks around, remembering the last time she was here. One day, when the time is right, she'll bring someone new with her.

This is the world she'll bring to her child to one day. A world of magic, adventure, and endless possibilities.

For now, though, she takes one last deep breath, savoring the feeling of the cool air against her skin, and then she climbs back onto the goose's soft feathers, ready to soar once more.

*The adventure has only just begun.*

The wind rushes through her hair, and Emma laughs, feeling contented.

People below look up and wave goodbye as she passes overhead, pointing and cheering at the royal sky riders.

It's like being a child again, but better. She's not just escaping into a story anymore; she's living it, weaving it on her own.

She'll be back, and just like always as Kesi taught her, all she has to do is close her eyes.

When she opens them, she's back in the library.

The world around her is still, the air filled with the familiar scent of old dusty weathered parchment. Emma sighs contentedly, running her hand over the closed book on her lap. She glances at the clock on the library wall, she knows it's time to go home. Emma feels something shift within her.

It was never about breaking the curse or just unlocking past memories, it was about preserving all these stories. Her mother's tales, the cursed crew's forgotten lives, all of it is connected to this place. A place of magic, stories, and knowledge. She realized with a deep certainty that the library wasn't just a gateway to worlds or a place where stories lived—it needed someone to be its guide and protect it.

It needed a librarian.

The truth settled over her like a warm blanket. The old librarian was gone for many years, and the library had been dormant. Her mother's stories had been a way of preparing her all along. Emma wasn't just on an adventure; she was meant to take on this role, to watch over the library, the books, the stories, and those who ventured into their worlds.

The island and the memories faded, but the understanding remained clear. One day soon, she would return to the library; not as a visitor, but as its guardian. And she has the key.

Emma stands, she hugs the book close to her as she makes her way through the library's endless aisles. She knows exactly where she's going, the path to the special section of the library etched in her mind after all these years.

When she reaches the farthest corner of the library, she finds a small table tucked away behind rows of dusty tomes. On the table sits a single, small book, bound in soft, worn leather, its pages glowing faintly with magic. It's not like the other books in the library. This one is special.

*It's for her child.*

Emma smiles as she picks up the book, feeling the faint pulse of magic within it. She knows that one day, when her child is old enough, they'll be ready to learn and read the secrets of the library and become the new guardian when the time is right.

And when that day comes, Emma will hand them this book, the key, and this library, a gift from the place that changed her life.

"Emma," Kesi calls from the entrance, his voice warm and full of love. But he still had the same mischievous voice that captivated her all those years ago. She smiles at herself, the images of the kingdom of Amaranth fading softly from her mind as she turns to see him standing by the arched doorway, his eyes gleaming with affection for her.

The years have softened the sharp edges of the boy who once stole the Eye of Horus. "It's time," he says, a smile tugging at the corners of his mouth.

Emma tucks the glowing book under her arm and  steps out into the cool evening air, Kesi's hand is outstretched for hers to hold, he gently kisses her cheek and lovingly pats her growing pregnant belly as the library's doors close softly behind them.

*The adventure of life isn't ever really over. It's just a continuation onto the next chapter.*

**Canadian Illustrator / Author Lizy J. Campbell** is a self-taught artist. She is a mother of two beautiful children and owns a publishing company and is an illustrator and painter. She has many interests including her new passion, crocheting!

"I love to create. There is no limit to what I want to do, so I keep reaching for the sky. I am enthusiastic about making a difference and making people smile, one creation at a time." – Lizy J Campbell

Liked the book? Please leave a review

www.ingramcontent.com/pod-product-compliance
Lightning Source LLC
Chambersburg PA
CBHW070352310726
48977CB00002B/419